SPRING SHOWERS

SARAH DRESSLER

5 PRINCE PUBLISHING
5PRINCEBOOKS.COM

Published by 5 PRINCE PUBLISHING & BOOKS, LLC

PO Box 865, Arvada, CO 80001

www.5PrinceBooks.com

ISBN digital: 978-1-63112-371-9

ISBN print: 978-1-63112-372-6

Cover Credit: Marianne Nowicki

04232024.1 04252024.2

To those who have experienced profound renewal after life's storms and to all the flowers for showing us that hope exists.

ACKNOWLEDGMENTS

I would like to thank my family for giving me the space to write, for inspiring me to follow my calling as a writer, and encouraging me to trust my instincts.

A huge thank you to my early readers, Racheal, Alesha, Becky, and Sarah. Your feedback and support means the world to me. This book would not be what it is today without you.

To my publishing team, my gratitude, for believing in me and helping to shape my stories. Thank you to Bernadette for your continued support. Cate, for your guidance through the editing process. And the rest of the team for bringing Spring Showers into readers' hands.

A special thank you to Original Lays, and the copious amounts of m&m's that I ate while writing this novel. I'm sure I could not have completed it without my comfort foods.

Lastly, to my readers, I am beyond thankful for you and your consistent enthusiasm to devour my sweet stories.

ALSO BY SARAH DRESSLER

SPRING SHOWERS

CHAPTER 1

Thandie swerved into the left lane, narrowly avoiding the crates of strawberries falling from the back of a pickup truck just ahead. Plump red globes spilled across the highway, slurping under her tires. The wheel wells of Thandie's car would be sticky for days. In her rearview mirror, bright green trees covered in cotton candy flowers whizzed by and she saw the truck driver finally pull to the side of the road. The driver's arm stretched out from the window and waved the traffic around.

"Whoa. Are you alright?" Davis asked through Thandie's phone speaker, since her car was too old to have bluetooth.

Thandie had nearly forgotten he was on the line. Why she had even answered his call after all these months was a question she would dig into later, but for now, she wanted nothing more than to find a reason to hang up on him. But his concern for her safety seemed genuine, so she didn't just yet.

"It looks like there was a murder on this highway," she said with a laugh.

"Ew, are you serious?" he said, not having grasped her sarcasm.

"Not an actual murder," she said and caught a glimpse of her

1

own blue eyes rolling in the reflection of the rearview. "A truck spilled strawberries all over the highway. It's red and splattered like blood."

Davis gave a humorless giggle. "I get it. The strawberries smashed, and it looks like roadkill or something. Funny."

Thandie hated that she always had to explain her jokes to him. It hadn't bothered her at first, but as their relationship progressed, he became more serious and she . . . Well, she would self-censor her banter before even saying her amusing thoughts out loud to him.

Thandie changed lanes back to the right. "Listen, Davis, my exit is coming up in a minute and I'll need to concentrate on the directions."

"Where are you heading?"

As far from you as I can get. "I'm going to start my new job near my friend JB, who I know from college. Do you remember me talking about her?"

His silence was his answer.

"Davis, I need to go."

"Wait," he said. "When can I see you?"

"Why would we need to see each other again?" Her words cracked as they came out of her lips with more hurt than she wanted him to be aware of. "Or did you forget what you did to me a few months ago?"

"Thandie, of course I didn't forget . . . I was just . . ." He paused, and she thought for a moment that he might actually be honest with her for once. "I had other things to take care of."

"Other things named Bianca?" Heat climbed up her neck. She tucked a stray brown curl behind her ear and took a deep breath before exploding at him. "You had real things to do. You had our rehearsal dinner. Oh, and that thing the next day. What was it again? Oh yes, our wedding!"

"Thandie, darling—"

"Don't you 'Thandie darling' me, Davis Mothan."

"I can tell that you're still upset—"

"That you deserted me the night before our wedding? You didn't show up at the rehearsal and then you called me that night, from Vegas no less, with no explanation. Huh, I wonder why anyone would be upset about that." Thandie removed her pink baseball cap and threw it to the seat beside her, where it landed in a pile of granola bar wrappers and empty water bottles. "Taking your call was a mistake. I need to go. I'm at my exit."

"Thandie," his tender pleading was tinged with something that sounded like remorse, but for Thandie, it was too little. "Will you please at least talk to me about it? I made a mistake, and you need to stop running at some point."

"You made it clear that I'm no longer your concern. Goodbye, Davis," she said and ended the call.

The notion of going back to him made her body shake. While he had slithered away back to Seattle, she had been on a seven-month-long journey eastward. Even if she made it to the ends of the North American continent, it wouldn't be far enough away from the man who had broken her heart.

The exit ramp narrowed, and the roadway dissolved into a rough grit. The car's tires skidded across the loose ground as she came to a stop sign. Looking both ways, she saw the crossroad was clear, and she creeped straight ahead. Around a hairpin turn, a weathered, gray, covered bridge with variegated vines and purple wisteria flowers dripping over the arched entrance came into view. If she hadn't been so antsy to get to The Foundry, she might have stopped and enjoyed the view of the quiet stream below. The riverbanks, painted with tiny wildflowers, stretched out in both directions beneath her.

Thandie took in as much of the lush scenery as she could while she inched her orange Geo Metro over the creaking road planks. On the other side of the covered bridge, the road became paved again, and a sign ahead showed the way toward

Elizabethtown and Christmas Cove. With her blinker set, she made for the Cove.

The view out of her window was nothing like back home, where corn stalks and grain silos dominated the horizon. This countryside, with its rolling hills and white steeples dotting the fields of flowers and newly green trees, felt like the change she desperately craved. A change that she hoped would take her mind off of all she had lost seven months ago when Davis selfishly derailed her future.

As though the universe read her thoughts, a church came into view as she rounded a bend in the road. On the top steps, just outside a carved wooden door, dozens of people gathered dressed in suits and pastel-colored dresses. At the bottom of the steps, an arch was decorated with hundreds of white and pink roses. Thandie could almost smell the flowers' essential oils drifting into the air.

Though the moment was a happy one for the lucky couple, whoever they were, sadness welled inside her heart at having missed out on having the wedding of her dreams, and she wiped her damp eyes. The church disappeared behind her car and she wondered if she would see herself wanting to get married ever again.

Coming around a bend, she found herself entering a thick and overgrown forest of towering pines. Sunlight filtered through the branches and soon enough gave way to a clearing. A green sign hung over the roadway announcing she was entering Christmas Cove. The speed limit dropped to ten miles per hour and the asphalt surface switched to a worn-down cobblestone that vibrated the car chassis. Slowing to the recommended speed, the jouncing lessened considerably.

Main Street was everything she had thought a quiet New England town should look like. A row of two- and three-story buildings stood sandwiched together and lined both sides of the street. Painted awnings provided shade and protected the glass storefronts, while the bay windows shimmered in the clear, late morning sun.

Upon closer inspection, she realized that many of the buildings were vacant, though there was a small shop that had a giant *Coming Soon* sign in the window. At the far end, a pink Victorian house was surrounded by scaffolding, and a dumpster on one side was overflowing with construction debris. Spring was blooming everywhere she looked, in the overgrown gardens, the cracks of the pavement, and even the window boxes hanging on an old gray house.

A right turn down a long, single-lane dirt road brought her to a large building that looked like a converted barn, though little remained of what a typical barn might look like other than the iconic shape. Charcoal-colored board-and-batten hugged the structure's exterior, with windows that stretched from ground to roof in wide intervals. Just inside, a dramatic crystal chandelier dangled from the high peak and reflected the sunlight back outside like glitter. At the entrance to the circular driveway, two granite pillars held a carved wooden sign that read, *The Foundry Retreat.*

CHAPTER 2

Grant gazed out the window at one impressive little tugboat bringing a large ship into Seattle's busy port. He tapped his fingers on the chrome edge of the desk in front of him, as though the action could somehow assist the tug. What it did was break the silence in the office. Quiet was not something he enjoyed. It often allowed too much room for his own thoughts to come through. Waiting was even worse. Now, he contended with both. A clock ticked and clicked from its place on a bookshelf, sounding in time with his pulse. Perhaps his pulse was matching the clock instead, but being a corporate consultant meant he was accustomed to operating on someone else's schedule. Working for different firms constantly meant sitting back and practicing his *patient* face.

Today, he happened to use the reflection in the glass of a framed photo sitting on the desktop to check on how his face was doing. Semi-convincing, as usual, though he felt his expression had improved slightly over the years.

Behind the glass was an image of a perfect and happy family, with two parents and three children wearing matching outfits and smiling with unusually white teeth. The watermark in the corner gave the phony family away. *Who keeps a photo of a fake family on their desk?* Grant wondered. The people's appearance in the stock photo may have been enhanced before the frame hit store shelves, but Grant's teeth were just as straight and just as white as theirs. His hair, on the other hand, was nowhere near perfect. It was a mess, like always.

No matter what he did to tame his thick, dishwater-blond waves, his hair would end up doing whatever it wanted, which was typically falling down on his forehead and tickling his brows. Leaning back into the semi-circular chair, he brushed his fingers back through his mop and propped his feet up on the edge of the desk.

Waiting. No matter the city, or what CEO's office he sat in, the delays were all the same. Never once had the other person been on time. But if he must wait, at least this office had a fantastic view. He gazed out the floor-to-ceiling windows and watched the ferry boats crossing Elliott Bay.

A shiny glass clock with its exposed gears dinged the hour, which meant his meeting was now half an hour behind schedule. He'd care more if he had anything better to do. He didn't know a soul in Seattle. He had no dinner plans, no museums to peruse, and no hot date to speak of, nor did he plan to stick around long enough to meet anyone.

Heavy footfalls vibrated in the hallway and approached his direction. Grant tore himself from his casual and reclined position, and straightened his spine just as the door opened behind his shoulder. Quickly, he aligned the photo frame where it had been, and stood up.

A man, about Grant's age but with much tidier hair, entered the office. His eyes were buried in his phone's screen, and he blindly reached out his hand towards Grant.

Grant shot his hand out, enthusiastic to make a good impression as he introduced himself. "Grant Goldie. It's a pleasure to meet you, sir." Their hands met and shook firmly.

"Call me Davis." He motioned for Grant to take a seat and finally looked up from his device. "I appreciate you coming in on a Sunday. But as you know, money doesn't take a day off." He laughed at himself.

"It's not a problem," Grant said.

Davis took a turn around the desk and paused at the window, looking down. "They're like little ants down there. Running back and forth, performing their little jobs, with no idea what it takes for people like us to keep it all going, you know?"

Grant did not relate. To him, money was just money. Sure, people needed a certain amount to live on, but more than that, he knew that money rarely made people happy. It turned out, he was just good with numbers. And reading people. Even so, in his business, he ran into many men like Davis who believed themselves to be the masters of the universe, so he replied, "Yep."

Davis grunted an agreement from his place at the window.

"Shall we get started?" Grant asked. "I got the package from your office, and I'm up to speed on the framework financials."

Davis took his seat with his back to the window. "I'm glad you could come out to Seattle and meet with me. I think it's important that we meet in person. Whether it's one dollar or a million, I need to see who I'm trusting, eye to eye. I don't take my ventures lightly."

"Of course you don't."

"I hear you're the best of the best when it comes to your analysis."

Grant was accustomed to his reputation preceding him, but it never got easier to accept the praise heaped upon him. "Well, I don't know if I'm the best but—"

"Humble, I like it. Good start," Davis said and continued his speech. "I'm looking at investing in a couple of boutique resorts on the east coast. I'm considering at least two properties as of now. I'm sure you read about it in the package my office sent over."

Grant nodded but couldn't get a word in.

"The one I'm having you go see is called The Foundry. I forget why they called it that, but it's a high-end retreat and there's nothing else like it in the area. Apparently there was a lake, which dried up some years ago. Recently, someone purchased many of the abandoned properties along the old shore. The retreat property can host a variety of different events throughout the year, which is what interested me in the first place. The Foundry can host seasonal retreats, wellness weeks, writing intensives, the options are endless really."

"But the owner needs the money to make it all happen?" Grant added.

"You got it," Davis snapped his fingers. "Someone I know is involved with the project, so I thought I might be interested in taking a look also. It's a quaint town and I've been on the hunt for something situated close enough to the city for people to utilize as a getaway. Plus, from what I hear, the owner has done a lot of work already. My point is, the place is set to open tomorrow, and I need you to be there. The goal here is to assess the long-term viability of the project. Even if I have other reasons for wanting to invest, it still needs to make financial sense. You'll need to investigate the property itself and make certain that you report on the staff—"

"Sir, I apologize for cutting you off, but I got this," Grant assured, though his impatience was showing. "This is what I do. I research the local area, see if the community can support a fluctuating population, and get a sense of the local support for the project. I'll look closely at the financials and the overall quality of the experience. People will pay if the value is there."

"Quite right. I trust you know what you're doing, which is exactly why I'm sending you there. You'll be a guest for the whole first week. With that in mind, I'm certain there will be some kinks for them to work out."

"Just so I know what to pack, what is the theme for this

week?" Grant asked and hoped it wasn't one of those kumbaya things about getting in touch with one's feelings and such.

"It's a wellness retreat. They've sent a preference sheet for you to fill out, but I'm sure you'll get a belly-full of granola and green smoothies," Davis said without humor. "I need you to pay special attention to the staff, and I expect a thorough report by the end of the week."

If there was one thing Grant was confident about, it was meeting a deadline. It was one way that his impatience was actually a benefit to him. Betterstill was his ability to sniff out the good from the bad. That's why he supposed his reputation had landed him the job in the first place. People wanted the best of the best when it came to spending potentially a million dollars or more, which begged the question . . .

"One more thing that wasn't included in the package. What is your proposed exposure with this venture?"

Davis seemed not to hear him at first. His face was buried in his phone again, and he refreshed the page he was on several times.

Grant cleared his throat just a little.

"Sorry, I'm so distracted. I've been trying to reach my . . . Well, a woman I was awful to. She's either screening my texts and calls or she's somewhere with no reception. Like, where in this country do cellphones not work?"

"I'm sure it's nothing—"

"Have you ever left someone at the altar, Grant?"

He shook his head and understood immediately why the woman may be screening her calls.

"I'm trying to make it up to her, if that's even possible." Davis flipped his phone face down on the desk and crossed his arms in front of his chest. "I'm willing to invest a quarter if you believe it's viable. And double it if you think it's a slam-run."

"Grand slam? Home run?" Grant corrected, but Davis only squinted at him with confusion pinching his face. The quarter

Davis referred to was $250,000, with an asterisk to double the investment to half a million upon Grant's positive assessment. The pressure was high for him to give an honest and thorough evaluation. "I understand what you're looking for and I'll have my report to you by week's end. Anything else?"

"My assistant has all your travel information." Davis pointed out into the hallway. "Have a nice trip."

CHAPTER 3

Pulling in beside a bright red pickup truck, the only other vehicle parked in front of the barn, Thandie got out of her car and checked herself in the driver's side window. She smoothed her frizzy ends into a fresh ponytail and shoved it all into her baseball cap. "That'll have to do," she said out loud with a nod to her reflection.

The huge barn loomed beside her. At the front, she was greeted by a wide glass and steel door that mimicked the lines of a common barn door. Raised cedar planters framed the door and overflowed with orange and yellow marigolds. The blackened wood siding gave off a sweet and smoky scent that reminded her of growing up on the farm.

As she reached for the long brass door handle, a man appeared through the other side of the glass with a friendly smile. She stepped back, and he swung the heavy door open for her. He was taller than he first appeared to be, and she found herself looking up at him when he spoke.

"You must be Thandeka Nkosi?" he said and shook her hand. "I've been expecting you. Was the drive in easy enough?"

"It was sticky," she said and pointed at the strawberry bits splattered across the hood and grill of her car. "I had a run-in with some escaped produce."

"Sounds eventful. Hopefully the rest of the week won't be so messy," the man said as they walked inside.

"Let's hope," she said and laughed nervously. "You can call me Thandie. And you must be Mr. Thorpe."

"Everyone calls me Leo, if that's alright with you." He showed her in past the service desk. "This is our meeting house." Leo swept his hand through the air quickly, but her eyes fixed on the massive chandelier hanging from the rafters twenty feet above them. "Meals are all served in here and snacks are provided throughout the day. That over there is the kitchen space." Leo pointed to a section of wall with a brass sign that read *Cucina*. Kitchen, in Italian.

Thandie nodded politely but she was unsure why she was being led on a tour instead of filling out employment paperwork or interviewing with the management team. Unsure of what else to do, she followed him towards the rear of the barn and listened.

"This area over here is our wellness and fitness center. There's a storage closet with all kinds of equipment. Most of the stuff can be used inside or outdoors if the weather cooperates. You'll have access to the entire grounds, and if there's anything you need, just let me or America know." Leo snapped his fingers and looked back at the front door. "She should be here by now."

Thandie turned and looked at whatever he was searching the space for. "Who?"

"Oh. America, my fiancée. If it weren't for her, I don't know if I would have been able to get this place going. Anyway, I came in early today to get some things sorted out and she was supposed to meet us here around lunchtime."

"You have a fiancée?" Thandie said. Just saying the word caused a shiver to vibrate down her spine, but she couldn't just let the question linger. "Congratulations. When's the big day? Sorry. You don't have to answer that."

"Don't apologize. You'll find out pretty quick that when you live in a small town, everyone knows your business."

Thandie knew all about that. Her hometown in Iowa was too small for just that reason. At least she believed that the town was too small following the wedding incident. It took about three and a half minutes for everyone in town to know what happened the night before her wedding. Despite the gossip mills, living in a small place wasn't all bad. There was always someone ready and willing to offer a helping hand, a cup of sugar, or some sage advice.

"Here she is now," Leo said and caught a running America in his arms. Their lips met, and he swung her around one time. Her dark hair came loose from the pile on top of her head and cascaded around her shoulder. Her feet hit the floor, one and then the other, like a dancer. The scene was straight off the set of a Hollywood rom-com.

Thandie giggled at the two lovebirds and hid her smile behind the back of her fingers. She couldn't help but note how good-looking the couple was together. He looked much like all the boys she had gone to school with in Iowa. Someone with northern European heritage and a ruggedness that came from knowing hard work. America was beautiful, with olive skin and a smile as wide as the sea. She looked as though she'd be home among the grapevines and Roman ruins of Italy. The couple reminded her of her own parents, the way they just looked like they were supposed to be together.

Hand in hand, the pair joined Thandie beside the *cucina*.

"I see you found our little kitchen," America said and pointed with her thumb. "Thandeka? I'm America."

"Nice to meet you. You can call me Thandie," she said as America hugged her. "Why is it called the *cucina*?"

"It was my mother's idea, the kitchen. The *cucina*. She's sort of obsessed with all things Italian after her trip to Tuscany a few months ago. Family history and all."

"I get that," Thandie said, though she didn't. She had little idea of her family history.

"Where are you from, Thandie?" America asked.

"Iowa," Thandie said. "But my parents are from South Africa and moved to the States before I was born."

"Do you ever want to go there?" America asked, but continued her own story before Thandie could answer. "I've never been to Italy, even though that's where my family comes from. Maybe someday I'll go check it out."

"Maybe you could go for your honeymoon. Mr. Thorpe tells me you're engaged," Thandie said. "Congratulations, by the way."

"It's Leo, please. And," he looked at America adoringly, "that's not a bad idea."

"I'll think about it," she said. "So, Thandie, what part of Iowa do you call home?"

"I'm from a tiny town—"

Leo squinted his eyes. "So, you *do* know about small towns?"

"Well versed."

"I think you'll fit in quite well here, and we're glad you could come help us out on short notice," Leo said. "I had mentioned the job to Jenny when I bumped into her a couple weeks ago and she said she knew just the person. And here you are."

"It's so funny to hear you call her Jenny. I've always called her JB," Thandie said. "We met during college, in North Carolina. She's the best. We keep in touch here and there, but I'll tell you, I was surprised when I got her call about this job out of the blue. It's as if she knew I needed it. I'm really looking forward to seeing her again."

America and Leo looked back and forth at each other and to Thandie with goofy grins and mischievous eyes. "Well . . ." America drew out the word like a drumroll.

"We have a surprise for you." Leo pointed over Thandie's shoulder, and she turned to see.

JB was a sight for Thandie's weary eyes, and she ran to meet her old friend at the door. "Jenny Bailey Townsend. It's been too long," Thandie said and wrapped her arms around her, patting something squishy on JB's back. "What happened?"

JB stifled a giggle in her throat as she unstrapped a long band at her waist and shoulders. Swinging her arms around like a trapeze artist, she retrieved the lump from her back and presented a baby. "This is what happened. Meet Charlotte Victoria Townsend."

Thandie loved babies. Perhaps it was part of getting older, not like twenty-seven years old was old, but she was old enough to know that she wanted to be a mother sooner rather than later. Perhaps there was still a wound left behind by her failed wedding to the man whom she had seen as a possible father to her future children. Or maybe she just knew that she was destined to be a great mom.

"May I?" Thandie asked. JB handed the baby over like she was passing off a ticking bomb, but Thandie was thrilled to take the baby. "She's precious. How old?" Thandie cooed.

"Six months next week. She was born right before Christmas, and not a day too soon." JB sniggered. "With how swollen my feet were and how much my back ached morning and night, I was ready for her to come into the world, you know what I mean?"

It was Thandie's turn to laugh. "I'm afraid I don't, but I can imagine all the same." Thandie handed Charlotte back to JB.

"How did I not know you were having a baby?"

JB recoiled from the question before answering in a hushed tone. "We didn't tell anyone this time around. It's too hard to have to call everyone back with bad news when it . . . you know?"

Thandie held her friend's hand. "Is that why you said you couldn't come to my . . . wedding," she whispered.

"A giant baby bump would give it away." JB looked at her baby with a kind of dreaminess in her eyes that Thandie guessed could only come with motherhood.

"I'm sorry I wasn't here for you more."

"Don't even worry about it. It's hard to keep up when we're thousands of miles away. But now you're here and we can catch up properly."

"I wasn't sure if I was going to see you this week. Thank you so much for getting me this job," Thandie said.

"I didn't get you this job. I only suggested it. You got the job and I'm sure you're going to be a big help. America and Leo are seriously the best, and they need a partner to help get this place off the ground." JB placed her free hand on Thandie's forearm. "Let's get together sometime next week, after you settle in around here."

Thandie's heart was full. Her mom had always professed that certain people would come in and out of her life at exactly the right time, and this was no exception. "Thank you, more than you know," Thandie said.

"Don't mention it. I have to get to the grocery store and back before this one's nap time," JB said as she opened the door with her free hand. "Good luck this week!"

Thandie waved goodbye to her friend, who she was glad was only a phone call away. Even though they didn't talk often, having a familiar face in a new town or at a new job counted for a lot. She waited for JB to pull out of the drive and turned back around. America and Leo were out of view.

"Hello?" she called out.

"We're in the *cucina*," America called back.

Thandie made her way around the wall and entered through a saloon-style door that swung both ways. America sat on a shiny silver workstation that ran down the center of the kitchen. From the stove to the wide refrigerator with glass doors, everything glistened and smelled of lemon-scented cleaning products. She doubted the kitchen had ever been used.

"She told me to keep her visit a secret," Leo said. "Probably in case something happened, and she wasn't able to make it over here. I'm glad it worked out for you."

"I appreciate it more than you know."

"So, where do you want to start?" America said while Leo busied himself making a plate of sandwiches.

"Honestly? I don't even know fully what the job is and what you expect. Maybe we should begin there?" Thandie said shyly. "All I know is I'll be the events coordinator for a wellness week retreat."

"You didn't tell her, Leo?"

"No, I thought you did," Leo said back with a playful tone.

"Tell me what?"

"You're in charge of the whole thing. The entire guest experience from the moment they arrive to the moment they leave," Leo said. "It'll be fun."

"Is that all? I could have used a few more days to prepare. Do I have any staff?"

"You're looking at it," Leo said.

Thandie had it in mind to bolt right then. But whatever the job required, she needed the paycheck. "So, what exactly do you need me to do?"

Leo took a platter filled with sandwiches out through the swinging door. "Come on," America said and led the way out to the dining area situated below the *cucina* sign. She handed Thandie a paper napkin. "I'm sure you're hungry after the drive. Grab one of these things and I'll take you to the office."

Thandie eyeballed the delicious-looking sandwiches. Multigrain bread was piled high with Vermont white cheddar, thin shaved turkey, tomatoes, and lettuce. Her mouth watered as she imagined biting into the best lunch she'd seen in days. "I'm so sorry. I can't eat this. I have celiac disease and can't have any gluten products." Thandie turned her eyes from the platter.

"Oh, don't worry. These are all gluten-free," Leo said with a smile about to break from the confines of his face.

"How . . . ?" she said and spied the sandwich she wanted.

"Jenny told us," Leo said. "And our chef has celiac disease too."

"So, the whole *cucina* is gluten-free. Isn't that great?" America clapped her hands with excitement.

Thandie picked up the sandwich she was sure she was drooling over and took a huge bite. Her eyes closed, and she savored the soft bread and fresh ingredients. Eating on a budget meant she usually didn't get to enjoy gluten-free bread. She took two more bites before finally coming up for air. "I don't know what to say. This is a fantastic surprise."

America threaded her arm through the crook of Thandie's. "That's what the chef said would happen. Now let's get to the office. I assume Leo showed you around a little before I got here?"

"He tried—"

America laughed. "That tracks."

"No." Embarrassment dripped from her lips. "I mean, we started to, then you came in. We didn't really have time for the whole tour."

"Relax. I'm only teasing you. And him. He likes it." America steered them to a narrow staircase that led to a loft area. "Here we are. The office. We just added this. Well, there was a loft here before, but I wouldn't say it was safe to walk on, let alone hold furniture and all these storage shelves. The whole barn has had an overhaul in the last eight weeks."

The loft was a wide-open space that covered about half of the barn's footprint. Rows of black metal storage shelves, like something one might see in a big-box store, held dozens of crates and bins. "What is all this?"

"You've got your different holiday decorations over there." America pointed to a grouping on one side. "And these are filled with things from binoculars to water slides, and ice skates and camping stoves. Pretty much anything you might need to put on any activity you can think of. You have access to anything in there."

"That's . . . thorough." Thandie said, suddenly seeing the scope of what they expected. "So, this week we have a wellness retreat?"

America flopped a large binder on the desktop.

"What is that?"

"This has everything you need to know for the week. All the guests' profiles, their preference sheets that include any limitations they have, and a sample schedule for you to start with. Of course, you should use it as a template and change it to whatever you think is best. Any questions?"

About a million, Thandie thought. "I think I can get something put together."

"The guests arrive tomorrow, and the retreat runs through Saturday," America said. "And then we'll figure out the next week."

"Is this like a trial run or something?" Thandie asked.

"Let's hope not. We already have bookings for the next few weeks," America said. "The one next week is another wellness retreat, so that should be easy to figure out. Then we have a writing retreat planned for the first of next month."

Thandie walked to the shelves and began taking stock of the items labeled on the bins. Some of the storage containers were made of clear plastic, and she could easily see the contents, while others were opaque and had detailed descriptions of what was stored inside. More than taking stock of the items, she was taking stock of the reasons for her staying there and managing such a massive job.

Her reason boiled down to necessity. She needed the money if she had any hope of moving on to the next place. Though she had only been there for an hour, she liked The Foundry so far. The thought of having to leave after only one week didn't seem as appealing as it had a few hours before. Thandie realized just how tired she was of running from one place to the next.

"Is everything alright?" America said from behind the desk where she was filing some papers.

"America, what's your story? I can tell you're not a small-town girl like me."

"What gave me away?" she joked and flicked her hair over her shoulder. "I was born and raised in the city until I came here last Christmas. I'm a writer and came here on assignment to write a piece about the town's amazing holiday celebration. But when I got here, the whole town was basically dead. There wasn't any Christmas for me to write about."

America's story got Thandie's attention. "What did you do?" Intrigued, she sat in a light-blue tufted armchair across the desk from America.

"I roped Leo into helping me bring back all the Christmas traditions so I could write my article. But instead of just finding a good story, I found my own Christmas in his kind heart and in the way we laughed together." America's eyes were distant and dreamy.

"So, you fell in love and decided to stay?"

"That's right. I knew this place was special, and I felt free here. Not like living in the city where the walls always seem to be closing in around you." America looked out of the floor-to-ceiling windows visible from the loft space, though she wasn't looking at anything in particular. "Enough about me. What's your story?" she finally said and looked at Thandie again.

"I'm just trying to move on from . . . from some bad stuff," Thandie said as she considered America's words.

"You know, sometimes starting over starts within," America said with no hint of judgment, only compassion. "I don't know what you're running from, but you have safe harbor here."

"Thanks for not pushing for more."

"You know what they say about small towns," America said and raised her brows in three rapid bursts.

"I'm aware." Thandie appreciated America's lightheartedness. Though they had only just met, Thandie didn't rule out the possibility that she could become good friends with America.

America closed the binder and folded her hands on the desk's worn wood surface. "Alright. Let's get down to it. What's your expertise and how can we use it this week?"

Thandie paused at that giant question. Her expertise? "I have a degree in botany."

"Hmm." America thought for a moment. "That could be useful if you take the guests out on the trails. What else?"

"Um, I don't have a fancy, over-priced piece of paper to back up this claim, but I'm stubborn and focused, and I don't like leaving a task undone. That's something, right?"

"That's a lot," America said.

"Not to sound rude, but it looks like you've already planned so much for the week. Why didn't you just handle this all by yourself?" Thandie asked, though she wished she had asked her question with a bit more tact.

"I'm a full-time writer, and honestly, I thought I could find the time and energy to take on helping Leo this week. But the truth is, a couple weeks ago, I realized that I couldn't do the job the way it needs to be done. Leo needed help, and he needed more focus than I could give him. It was my pride stopping me from asking for help earlier. Now I know better."

Thandie nodded in agreement, though a pang of guilt twisted in her. Pride was the reason she had been on the run for seven months. Pride had stopped her from leaning on her friends and family when she had really *needed* someone to lean on. Now, pride was pushing her down a path of endless random jobs and half-acquaintances.

"Well, I'm glad to be here for now. I'm grateful to you and Leo for giving me the chance," Thandie said. "You two seem really great together."

"He's pretty lucky to have me." America giggled. "All kidding aside, I'm happy you're taking this job on. And honestly, anything you can do to keep this week on track will be better than nothing. You'll be just fine. Now that we have all our pleasantries out of the way, how about I show you to your cabin?"

"I get my own cabin?" Thandie said.

"Of course. You're the employee of the month, didn't you hear?"

"I'm your only employee."

"Never mind the details. We're just glad you're here."

CHAPTER 4

Although small towns were not foreign to Thandie, a breathtaking panoramic view was. Home was where white dirt roads cut through the landscape like arrows straight to the heartland, and sturdy corn stalks, topped with golden plumage, stood in tight rows like soldiers on watch. Here, the roads snaked around endless hills, and through narrow valleys. Handcrafted bridges made long before her hometown in Iowa was ever thought of, spanned streams and creeks as old as time itself. She wondered if she would ever tire of the gorgeous view from The Foundry's barn.

Following slightly behind America, Thandie walked down the gravel drive from the barn with her luggage in tow and a twenty-pound binder in the crook of her arm. The drive tapered into a single lane pathway that looked to have been recently resurfaced with white and gray crushed stone. Along the edge of the path, bright green grass had recently been cut back and smelled of that moist, citrusy warmth of warmer days.

Beside the path, a split rail fence ran down the gentle slope and separated the road from a dry streambed. Up ahead, and about 300 yards from the barn, a cabin's white metal roofline came into view from behind a grouping of trees and shined in the afternoon sun.

Beyond the cabin, a large flat plain stretched out as far as she could see. Tufts of colorful wildflowers and tall grasses saturated the expanse, and, at the bottom of the hill, the path ended at what looked like an old dock or a broken bridge.

"Pretty spectacular, isn't it?" America stopped and asked as she herself took in the view.

"It's pretty breathtaking. The guests will fall in love," Thandie said as she breathed in the aromatic air. "Is it always like this?"

"I'm not sure," America said. "We had a really wet and warm winter. And you know what they say?"

Thandie looked at her blankly. "No rain, no flowers?"

America giggled. "Spring is a lovely reminder of how beautiful change can be."

Thandie considered America's words. "Yeah," she said as she counted the colorful species.

"I hope this never gets old. This is my first spring here and I'm loving it so far."

Thandie nodded and smiled. "I can see why. All we get in Iowa this time of year is dirt plumes from all the plowing." She pointed to the bottom of the hill. "What is that down there?"

"Oh, that. This used to be a lake. I thought you knew."

Thandie shook her head, and they resumed walking down the path.

"There was a dam downstream for nearly a hundred years, but it gave way during a big storm a few years back. You know how it goes. Town builds a dam. People fall in love with the town. The dam breaks. People break up with the town when the lake dries up . . . You know?"

"Drying up, just like my love life," Thandie said under her breath.

America did a double take, having obviously heard the

remark, and stifled a giggle. "Sounds like you have a story of your own there."

"Maybe so, but the one about the dam sounds way more interesting. Is that why you and Mr. Thorpe are starting this retreat? To bring people back to the town?"

"For the last time, you can call him Leo," America said. "Anyway, The Foundry was his idea at first, before I even knew him, but with my connections at the travel magazine, we were able to advertise this as a destination locale and get the retreat off the ground."

"What magazine do you write for?" Thandie asked and wondered whether she had read any of America's articles before.

"Jet Trek. Have you heard of it?"

"Yeah. It's an online publication, right? I think I see little clips now and again on the gram."

"That's great, I'll have to let the social team know their posts are cutting through the din." America clapped. "So, with some gentle coaxing from me and Leo's friend, Pa, we went all in and used the rest of his inheritance to buy the properties and outfit the place." Beneath her perky and controlled exterior, Thandie sensed a sort of desperation.

"Who's Pa?"

"You'll meet him at some point. He's always lurking around."

"Should I be worried?" Thandie asked nervously.

"Not at all. He's great, and he's been in this town forever. If I can't get you what you need, he can."

"Good to know," Thandie said as they came to the front of the cabin facing the old lake.

White painted steps led up to a wide wraparound porch. Two rocking chairs and a wrought iron side table sat in front of a set of three tall and narrow windows. A barrel planter made from an old wine cask greeted her on the other side of the porch. America held the door and let Thandie go in first. "This is all for me?"

Walking into the space, Thandie breathed in the thick scent of cedar, which is where the cabin's rustic feel ended. America headed straight for the contemporary style kitchen with white cabinets, complete with stone counters and high-end appliances.

"Your fridge is stocked with some essentials, and if you need anything else, just get it from the *cucina*," America said and pointed across the room. "That's the living area. The fireplace works, just flip the switch on the wall. That's the bedroom and bathroom through that door there."

"This is amazing." Thandie took in the sight of the beautiful wood logs, stacked and cemented together, and smelling of earth and warmth. Lightweight white curtains hung at the windows where daylight illuminated the entire vaulted great room, and the modern kitchen looked to be everything and more that she would need to feel at home there. "This cabin is so nice. Shouldn't it be for the guests?"

"Of course not, this cabin is closest to the barn, which is easier for you to get to. And all the guest cabins are down by the old shore. We were able to purchase the old lake houses for a bargain."

"I can bet." Thandie said and realized her comment overstepped her position. "Sorry. I didn't mean to imply—"

"It's fine," America assured her. "You'll discover quickly that we don't let things ruffle our feathers much. Plus, you're right. With the town basically deserted, no one wanted the structures. We may be the only people foolish enough to take on such a project." America paused and took a deep breath. "We really need this week to go off without a hitch."

Thandie's suspicions were confirmed in the tone of America's voice. Although the woman sounded relaxed, there was an undercurrent of anticipation and hope in the way she wanted everything to be perfect. A desperation that smacked of worry.

"I'm here to do my best," Thandie reassured. "I won't let you down."

She took a look around the beautiful, welcoming space and

thought about all the random places she had stayed and the other jobs she had taken over the last few months. Gratitude filled her heart to be somewhere so inviting and lovely.

"I should let you get started planning the week. There's a phone beside the bed and you can ring the office if you need anything," America said and let herself out the front door.

Even though Thandie had been sitting in the car all morning, she flopped right into the worn leather sofa and kicked her feet up on the coffee table. She wasn't tired, but she let her eyelids shut for a moment while she let her mind do the work of planning the week.

She didn't know much about wellness retreats, though the irony wasn't lost on her that practically all of her friends had suggested she go to one following the wedding incident. Perhaps she should have taken their advice, seeing as how she was now charged with putting one on herself. The wellness of a dozen guests was in her inexperienced hands. Though there was no reason to think she would outright fail, there was a learning curve to every job, and she had but a few hours to get a plan together before the guests were scheduled to arrive.

She had been the co-chair of her sorority's planning committee, which meant that she could organize just about anything with enough time. But time was something she did not have. And it seemed that her future at The Foundry depended on having a successful week with her playing the part of the best director that she could be.

Leaning over, she reached for the binder. The freshly printed pages, crisp and white, held the key to her planning. She flipped through the preference sheets and looked for any relative threads that connected one person to another.

All but two of the guests were physically able to go on mild hikes. No one was opposed to swimming, which was of no consequence, since there was no water around that she was aware of. The guests' ages ranged from their mid-thirties to some older folks in their sixties. The older ones might want to turn in early or participate in different activities, so she decided to plan a variety of events throughout each day.

Her first thought was to offer the guests a list of options during their check-in and, depending on the weather, choose the activity that best suited them. As long as she announced the next day's schedule at dinnertime, the guests would have enough time to prepare, and she would gain the bit of flexibility that she would need to get the week going.

But her plan didn't account for the first day. She needed one activity ready to go. Something not too hard, and one that people would be ready to do right away after check-in.

Thandie took her phone from her back pocket and opened the browser. A little circle chased its tail for a moment until a pop-up informed her there was no data connection. She closed and reopened the app, reset her wifi, and checked her signal strength, but there was nothing.

"Shoot," she said and tossed her phone aside. She had planned on doing a bit of research, looking up points of interest on the map, and getting some idea of the property's layout. Now, she would have to do it the old-fashioned way and go see things with her own eyes.

Heading outside, she recalled seeing a sky-blue painted bicycle leaning against the side of the front porch railing. It didn't take long for her to get back to the barn, which was slightly uphill from her accommodations, and park the bike in the rack underneath a covered stall. She wondered if all the cabins had likewise been outfitted with bikes, something she would ask Leo or America about when she found them.

The barn—Thandie decided it needed a better name—was quiet inside. The lights were low, as if on a motion sensor, but as she walked further into the space, the lights did not illuminate beyond their initial appearance. Perhaps the fixtures were tied to the outside light or set on a timer depending on the time of day to account for the natural light flooding the spectacular wall of glass. The light coming through the windows bounced off the crystal chandelier hanging in the center of the vaulted ceiling and sprinkled glittering rainbows about the cozy velvet couches and lounge chairs below.

"Hello?" she called out, breaking the calm ambiance. "Mr. Thorpe? Leo?"

No one answered, but she heard what sounded like a murmur of voices coming from the *cucina*.

Not wanting to frighten anyone, she knocked on the door to the prep area. The voices were unchanged, so she pushed the door open slowly just a crack and peeked in. The chef, wearing a tall white hat and matching white coat, hunched over the stainless-steel countertop, chopping away, and prepping vegetables. The man was mostly hidden behind long strands of fresh pasta hanging from coat hangers above the prep area.

Something simmered and steamed on the stove, and the chef flipped the sauteing meat into the air before catching it all again without spilling a morsel. That's when Thandie saw the headphones in his ears. He was speak-singing the lyrics to whatever song was playing, though she couldn't make out what the tune or even the language of the song was.

She'd meet the chef later. No need to interrupt what was clearly a great workflow, and besides, she needed to find out about the internet signal or wifi. She needed to find the people in charge.

It only took her a moment to check the dining area and the meeting space. The fitness area was deserted too. As she passed the stairs, she figured she would check in the office. If nothing else, she could take a closer look at whatever items were at her disposal for use the next day, and she might even get a few ideas depending on what she found.

As she approached the top stairs, America and Leo's voices became clear. They were whispering intently about something, and Thandie thought it was best to come back later. That was until she heard them say her name, which held her feet in place.

Her interest was piqued. She sat down a couple steps from the top where she was hidden from their view by a pony wall and listened. Eavesdropped.

"Don't you think we should tell her?" America said. "She's so sweet, and Jenny told us we could trust her."

"I don't want her to get all weird about it," Leo said. "You know how important this week is. I've spent the last of my inheritance on this venture. And I need the investor to buy in."

"But I think she can help—"

"I think she should just focus on her job. And we should focus on ours. You have an article to get to. I have all this, and it's a lot," Leo said. "Which is exactly why I need the investment. I can barely afford to pay her as it is. And if this doesn't go well . . ."

Great, just fantastic. Another job, another place to move on from. It sounded like even if she did a wonderful job with the retreat, her fate was really in the hands of some investor.

Thandie stood up to leave, and the stairs creaked so loud, she was certain the chef down in the *cucina* probably heard it too. "Shoot," she whisper-yelled and tiptoed down the steps, hoping no one noticed.

"Thandie," America's voice sounded from the top step behind her back.

She froze like a statue, squinting her eyes as though maybe she was temporarily transparent.

"Did you need something?" America said.

Apparently, Thandie was entirely visible. And caught.

CHAPTER 5

Thandie turned around slowly and looked at America standing at the top of the steps. Leo's head poked out over the pony wall with a narrow smile cutting across the lower half of his face.

"How much did you hear?" America said.

"Enough," Thandie admitted. "I wasn't being sneaky. I was coming to ask about the wifi and . . ."

America walked down the steps. "The internet and cell signals are spotty around here."

"We're working on it," Leo added. "Let's go sit in the dining room and talk. I think it's time we get on the same page."

They sat at three sides of a small square bistro table. A jar sat in the middle where a centerpiece might go. Instead of flowers, this one held individually wrapped breadsticks. She eyed the lightly toasted bread and her mouth watered.

"I told you before, everything here is gluten-free." Leo pointed at the sticks.

She didn't hesitate and took one from the jar. As she unwrapped the plastic, Leo explained. "I'm out of money. That's the truth. I'd been praying for a miracle when a venture capitalist contacted me out of the blue about a week ago, wanting to invest in the project. I'm not even sure how he knew about this place, but the firm is sending a representative to conduct an assessment during the retreat this week."

Thandie swallowed a half-chewed bite of the crunchy bread and cleared her throat. "So, if you don't get the investment, this place is done? Just like that?" Thandie asked and took another bite.

"Not necessarily," America said. "We can limp along through the summer, and hope things pick up enough, but we won't be able to expand the way we need to in order to be able to offer all the luxe, high-end amenities that we envisioned. As it is, everyone in town has pitched in their time and resources as much as they can, but it's still not enough."

"And my job is expendable," Thandie said and knew that she was correct. "It's just pure business. I can get things going this week, and you both can fill in the gaps once I'm gone." Disappointment dried her mouth like it was filled with cotton balls. "I was just getting to like this place, you know."

America and Leo shifted their eyes to each other as though they were experiencing a whole conversation without speaking a single word aloud. A nod back and forth and a grin later, America spoke. "What are *you* not telling *us*?" America asked.

"It's nothing." Thandie realized she dismissed the question too quickly to be believed. "Fine. If we're doing a whole *being honest* thing."

"We are," America and Leo said together.

"Do you always do that?" Thandie joked and got a shrug in response. "The truth is, I need this job. Like a lot. And I was hoping it would be for at least the season, through the summer."

"I would love to tell you that is the plan. You've barely started here, and I can sense that you're a great fit for the kind of atmosphere I want to create here. I just can't promise you anything right now," Leo said, and Thandie could tell he was being genuine.

"I understand, I really do. I'm grateful for the chance to work here, and—since we're being honest—one paycheck is better than none."

"Does that mean you'll stay on through the week?" America clapped her hands together. "Please say you will."

The arrangement would benefit everyone. If she did an excellent job, the investor would be happy, and the retreat could expand and stay open, which would mean she could keep her job. But it wasn't what she thought she had signed up for, and twenty minutes earlier she had actually imagined herself staying for a while. That looked like a long shot now.

"So, you'll stay?" Leo repeated America's query.

This was it. Did she give The Foundry her all and stay on for a while, or did she limp back to her hometown and beg for whatever charity her friends or family were willing to dole out until she got on her feet again? The latter sounded terrible. Admitting defeat wasn't something she felt up to.

"I don't really have a choice. I have no money to go anywhere else," she said. "It looks as though we three are in this boat together now. Let's just hope it doesn't sink us all."

"I know I didn't press earlier, but this is a small town and I'm bound to find out at some point. Can I ask about your situation?" America said and placed her hand on top of Thandie's as though she sensed her need for compassion. "Jenny didn't really say. She only said you could use the work and that you'd be a terrific addition to our little enterprise."

"I do need the work. I've blown through my savings over the past few months, though it wasn't much." Thandie looked at Leo. "I suppose we have that much in common. I was stood up the night before my wedding and I've been running ever since. The son of a . . . He just left town. Didn't even say goodbye or give me a reason."

"I'm so sorry. What a low thing to do."

"I had to get out of there. I was humiliated in front of the entire town and had nothing to keep me there. I was planning a life with a man who didn't have the decency to look me in the eye and tell me he was done." Tears pushed at the back of Thandie's eyes and for the life of her, she refused to let one more drop fall on his account.

"It's alright, you can let it out," America said and came around to put an arm around Thandie's shoulders.

"No," she said, and America pulled back probably thinking she was being scolded for the hug. "Sorry, it's not you. It's just, I'm tired of crying about this. The next time I cry it's going to be because I am the happiest person in the world. It will be for something good, not something bad."

America gave her a hug like a sister would and looked her straight in the eye. "If we all work together this week, maybe we can make that happen. Are you in?"

"I don't really have a choice. But that's not why I'll stay. You both have welcomed me here and have been nothing but great so far. JB—Jenny—vouched for me to have this job, and I want to help you succeed."

She pulled her tears back from the brink as she steeled her resolve to stay and do the best job she could for The Foundry. What was, would never be, and there was no looking back at what could have been. That part of her life, the one with Davis as her husband, a cute house, and a cat, and a happy-ever-after was behind her and the only way forward was ahead.

"I'm sorry we weren't truthful at first, but I hoped it wouldn't need to come up," Leo said. "Ideally, the week would go great, and we would get the money. You'd never need to know things were precarious. But now that you know, I'm sort of relieved."

"Who else knows?" Thandie said and looked around, though they were alone, save for the noises coming from the *cucina*.

"My parents. They live in town now," America said.

"And Pa," Leo added.

"Which means that Carol probably knows too," America said as they counted off on their fingers.

"Who are they?" Thandie asked and took another bite of the bread stick.

"Edwin, we call him Pa. I was telling you about him earlier," America said. "And Carol is the gatekeeper around here. She's been a fixture in these parts forever and knows everything about everything, you know?"

"I get it. My hometown has a few hundred people, but since most of them are farmers, they live scattered around the little main street. There's a lady that lived across the street who was like your Carol. Love her or hate her, she's sort of the glue that holds everything together."

"That's our Carol," Leo said. "Other than her, I don't think anyone knows the full extent of the situation."

"So, who is this person coming to check out the place?" Thandie asked.

"We don't know. It's one of the guests this week, but for obvious reasons, we don't know anything about him or her. You can see why," Leo said.

Thandie coughed on a dry crumb.

"Do you need a drink?" Leo asked.

She nodded.

Leo walked to a sideboard and poured a glass of water from a pitcher. "If we knew who it was, the experience might be altered to suit the investor, and not be an authentic experience. As it is, the fact that we know he or she will even be here this week has already changed our focus more than it should."

"By hiring me?"

Leo nodded and handed her the water glass. "You need to treat everyone the same. Don't be an investigator and try and figure it out. Just do your job. Keep all the guests happy and active, and I think everything is going to work out. I didn't get into this blindly. I know this concept for hosting rolling retreats all year round is sound. There's a market wide open for a place where people can connect to their interests with other like-minded people. It's going to work."

"It's going to work," Thandie agreed. "I suppose I have some prepping to do. This week isn't going to plan itself."

CHAPTER 6

Thandie woke early. The sun hadn't yet come up, but the pale-yellow sky glowed just beyond the white sheer drapes that hung at her bedroom window. As she lay, stretching her muscles and waking up her joints, she replayed and picked apart her first day there. Yesterday had been far from what she had expected, but it made the top of the list for the most exciting first day of work she'd ever had.

There was no smooth onboarding. No shoes, big or small, to fill. No real plan to speak of. And only a narrow chance that she'd still have a job come next week. Her future was quite literally in her own hands. She was in a make-or-break moment and was aware that the added pressure could work in her favor. The stakes were high, with Leo and his retreat hanging in the balance between her performance and an investor's whim.

This week wasn't going to be easy, but she could do everything in her power to create the best wellness retreat that Christmas Cove had ever seen.

After her talk with Leo and America, Thandie had gotten right to work and used the computer in the office to pull a ton of ideas together from the web. There were more options available to her than she had time or manpower to implement, but she would try what she could.

Thandie decided to start her day off the right way by making her bed. It was a shame the way she had flopped onto the supple mattress last night and kicked all the extra pillows right onto the floor. Seeing it made so neatly to start with, she made a note to find the expert who had done such a nice job with the linens and ask for some pointers. If she could replicate the tight sheets, the smooth corners, and the right amount of cushiness, she could have as restful a night's sleep every night, no matter where she was staying. She hadn't slept so well in longer than she could remember. At least not since the evening of the terrible, horrible, no good, very bad rehearsal dinner.

She was glad the kitchen was stocked with some essentials. A bright yellow banana paired perfectly with an almond biscotti for a quick breakfast. As it was a workday, she threw on her favorite light brown cargo pants, a white tank top, dark brown New Balance sneakers, and a white baseball hat that she had owned for years, though she had no clue when or where she had gotten it. She tucked her curls up under the hat and pulled her signature ponytail through the hole.

Grabbing her notes from the previous night's brief research session, she headed to the barn to gather supplies. It was a nice short bike ride to the barn, which she still thought deserved a better name. Naming the dining area the *cucina* was so cute, but *the barn* didn't sound cool enough for a place like this. She thought of different options on her way. *The main house, the big house, or the clubhouse all sound a little too generic*, she thought and parked her bike under the covered bay.

Looking out over the dried-up lake, she sniggered. "The boathouse," she said out loud.

"What's that?" Leo's voice sounded from behind her and caused her to jump.

"Nothing," she said and tucked a piece of errant hair behind her ear. "I was just thinking of different names we could call the barn. It's stupid."

"The barn is stupid?" he laughed.

Embarrassment heated her cheeks. "No, not the barn. Me trying to come up with a new name for it. The barn is fine. It's good even. Right on the nose."

"I'm only teasing." Leo opened the large door. "I think it's a good idea to give this place a proper name. We've called it the barn for so long it just kinda stuck. But you're on to something. It should have more purpose. What did you say out there? The boathouse?" He laughed.

"Yeah. I just saw the old lake and the name just flashed in my mind. It's kinda silly though, since there's no water anymore."

"I'll put it on the short list," Leo said without sarcasm, which she appreciated. "Did you come in for breakfast?"

"No, I ate a little bit back in my cabin. Thank you for stocking the supplies. If I stay on, I'm happy to purchase my own groceries though," she said as they moved further into the space. Thandie wasn't sure which one of them was leading the way, they both sort of hummed along beside each other, and she supposed they were each intending on visiting the office loft.

"Can I . . . I mean, is there something you needed in *The Boathouse?*" he waved his hands in front of his chest. "That doesn't sound right, does it? We'll keep thinking on it."

"I'll let you know what else I come up with. In the meantime, I was hoping to print some things off and add a map of the local area. I want to mark the landmarks and trails for the guests."

Up in the loft, Leo dug around in a bin stacked next to the desk. "I think I have a map that shows some walking trails. Would that get you started in the right direction?"

She nodded. "Also, I was thinking that if this place takes off, having an app that guests could download would be pretty useful. We could load their individual schedules and activity

SPRING SHOWERS

information right on to it. There'd be no guesswork involved for them, nor for whoever fills my current role in the future."

"I love that idea." He snapped his fingers. "For this week, the printer here works just fine if you just need plain paper, but if you need something more, you may have to go into Elizabethtown. And as for the app, the internet works well enough with the old-school wire in the wall, but not well enough to have the guests rely on it yet."

"It was just an idea."

"It's a good one," he said. "Now where is that map? It's not in this one." Leo walked the length of the loft and read the tags on the bins. His finger tapped each one as he passed it. "America and Carol did all this. I know there's a logic to the way it's organized, but I haven't figured it out yet."

Thandie joined the effort from the other end. "What are we looking for?"

"Look for something labeled maps, though I doubt it will be that easy." Leo chuckled.

The first section of tubs and boxes were labeled with things like jump ropes, s'mores, and flashlights. The next row featured labels such as Christmas – Lights, and Christmas – Red Ornaments, or Fall – Pumpkin Signs. The next row over was probably the one she needed. With no large bins, the shelves were filled with small file boxes that were ideal for map storage.

"Here it is." Leo said and pulled out a file box from the other side of the shelf in front of her. His face found the hole and looked through the gap at her.

"How do you know?" she asked.

"It says *Maps*."

"Of course it does." She giggled.

Leo removed the lid and placed it on the desk beside the computer screen. He fingered through dozens of maps and pulled one out. "Not it," he said and handed it over. "Though it might be useful."

41

Thandie turned it over and unfolded it fully into a three-foot-by-three-foot map of the area. Dozens of points of interest were marked with colored dots. In the bottom left corner, a key described what each colored dot represented. "Floristic realms. This is a map of flowers. How cool!"

"I thought you'd like that," Leo said.

"I got it." Leo unfolded his map and turned it around for Thandie to see. "This is us, right here," he pointed. "This is Elizabethtown. Technically we are part of Elizabethtown now, but we still call this place Christmas Cove. So anywhere on the map that's inside this shaded area is what I would consider local. This area over here is what I would consider no-man's-land."

"That sounds ominous," Thandie said, wanting to know more. "Is there something I should know?"

"Not really. My brother John is the mayor of Elizabethtown, which, as I said, we are now part of, and I like to keep as much distance between him and me as possible. Plus, if he knows what we're trying to build here, he'll probably try and find a way to ruin it all." Leo looked up as though he could see through the rafters. "Just stay in the shaded area, okay?"

"I got it."

"Let me know if you need anything. I've got things to do before the guests arrive in a couple hours." Leo grabbed a few papers off the desk and headed down the stairs.

Thandie got right to work unloading things from the bin labeled Hiking. There were extendable poles for stability, and red, wide-brimmed bucket hats that would be good for easily spotting wayward guests. She grabbed small binoculars and about a dozen canteens. Using the printer, she scanned the section of the map that correlated to The Foundry and made thirty copies. She hoped it wasn't wishful thinking that she would have another retreat to host, but figured either way, someone else could use any leftover maps.

Downstairs, she rearranged three of the small square tables

and set up a welcome zone for the guests. There was a check-in desk at the front beside the *cucina*, but this would be the activities area, she decided. On the table, she laid out the various hiking paraphernalia and fanned out the maps.

That's when she realized she needed to go walk to the trail before the guests' arrival. She took the top copy and a walking stick and set off towards the shore and the trailhead.

The trail followed along the dry streambed for a hundred yards before crossing over an old stone bridge. The path traced the old shoreline for a while and hooked around another unused dock-to-nowhere. She noted that it would be a great place for the guests to rest if needed before heading up the next leg. A steep, short incline led up to a lush overlook paved with red bricks and hemmed in by a rotten wooden railing. She snapped some photos of a weathered bench seat that needed some repairing if this trail was going to be more heavily used going forward.

Looking down the hill, she spotted the same unused dock that she had passed. It would make an ideal waiting area for those who didn't want the extra challenge of hoofing it up to the lookout. Those guests could wait while the others continued up to the incline. The hike, she hoped, would make for a perfect first day of the retreat. Guests would be free to join the hike, at a difficulty level they were comfortable with.

Later, after supper, she planned to host a welcome bonfire on the old shore. Near the defunct dock, there was a ring of large stones and a pile of wood made up of cut logs and raw, fallen branches.

Pleased with the plan, Thandie brushed the dust from her pants and headed back to the barn. She wished she had taken the bicycle instead of walking the whole thing; it would have given her an idea whether the trail was suitable for biking or not, though she felt it could be.

Back at the barn, she passed her bike right where she had left it by the entrance and went inside to the office. She needed to print out the day's schedule, add it to the activities desk, and arrange the rest of the hiking gear.

"Thandie, are you up there?" America's voice called from downstairs.

"Up here," she said and heard America run up the steps.

"I'm here to help," America said with a smile and bright eyes. "I had to get some writing done this morning, but I'm free the rest of the day."

"Thank you. I'm happy to have the help."

"Put me to work," America said and plopped down in the chair across from Thandie. "You look like you belong there. Like a boss girl."

Thandie shyly nodded.

"You don't seem the corporate type, though," America noted. "Remind me what your job was before this."

"My degree is in botany. It's very useful on the farm, but doesn't really translate into many other employment opportunities, if you know what I mean."

"Just because you have a degree in something, doesn't dictate what you have to do for the rest of your life. Look at me. I was an editor for a travel magazine for years. Now I have my own feature in each issue where I get to shed light on untouched places around the country. I get to write every day, and if you had told me this six months ago, I would have laughed in your face." America crossed her ankles and folded her arms like whatever she was about to say was the final word. "You're allowed to change course in life, as often as you want until you find something worth sticking around for."

Thandie considered her words and thought of how hard she had been running away from her humiliation, but not towards anything in particular. "It's hard to move on sometimes."

"Sometimes, you have to wipe the past clean before you can move forward."

"And sometimes . . . " An image of Davis falling off a cliff flashed in her mind. She shook the terrible notion and cracked a smile. "You have to find something worth moving towards first."

"Touché," America nodded. "Now, what's on your list?"

"Um. I need to check the accommodations." Thandie stood.

"Done."

"What do you mean?"

"I did them all yesterday before you arrived. Do you want to see them?" America said and sported a very proud grin. "Come on, I'll show you. Do you want to grab a snack first?"

"Yes, to both."

Downstairs, they stopped by the *cucina*, where a platter of sandwiches and fresh fruit and cut vegetables sat on a sideboard, buffet style. America led the way and took one of the paper-wrapped sandwiches. Thandie followed suit.

They ate as they walked down to the cabins that lined the old shoreline and looked out on the vibrant, wildflower-covered plain. America pointed out the name of each cabin and explained a bit of their history. The Round House had a curved deck at the back. The A-Frame was simply that. The Silver was named after the family that had owned it. The Carol was a slightly crooked log structure, and the Bear Cabin was in an open space nearest to Thandie's cabin.

Towering pines and bright green maple trees shaded the cabins and pathways below. Philadelphus shrubs with tiny white flowers bloomed all around and released an intoxicating sweetness, reminiscent of ripe oranges, into the air. Thandie wondered if she would ever tire of the serene view.

The path connected all the cabins back to the barn, and she spotted several quiet areas for some activities. A gazebo sat on a little rise and looked big enough to hold a dozen people for a yoga class or journaling session. A bench sat under a cherry blossom tree, where little pink flowers fell like snow to the ground around it. And then there was the old dock with a flagpole standing tall at one corner. The American flag waved with the breeze and reminded her of the corn plumes in late summer back home. The landmark could serve as a good waypoint for anyone venturing off the beaten path, and the guests could find their way back to the property.

Thandie and America walked the whole area and ended up back at the barn. *The lodge? No,* she thought, *that doesn't seem right either.*

CHAPTER 7

Noon. Right on schedule, a parade of cars drove over the hill towards the barn, leaving a wake of dust spreading into the sky behind them. One by one, the vehicles pulled into the undefined parking spaces on the north side of the barn.

Standing outside the doors, Thandie plastered a smile and opened her eyes very wide, knowing her expression would settle nicely into a bright and alert state. Why was she nervous? These guests were just people, like herself, who needed a break from whatever was going on in their life that needed breaking from. She let the nerves course through her before shaking the feeling off.

The first car door opened. A very tall woman stepped out of the car. Her blonde hair was grown-out, revealing gray roots, and it hung in stringy clumps of mixed texture. It reminded Thandie of the reason she preferred ponytails and caps most days for taming her own hair. From the passenger side, another woman emerged, shorter and full-figured, and laughing.

Thandie approached the cars. Her intention was to greet the guests personally, but the side effect was overhearing whatever the two women had just been jesting about. Thandie was a sucker for a good joke, and she wanted badly to feel free to laugh so hard again.

From the binder that America had prepared, Thandie knew all their names and bios, but had no face-to-name recognition. And for the life of her, she couldn't help but wonder which one of the guests, or perhaps it was a couple, was sent there to spy for the investment firm.

"Good day, ladies," Thandie said as she approached the rear of the first vehicle. "Head inside where you can check-in and enjoy some refreshments. I'm glad you made it to The Foundry safely."

From the next car, two couples, separated by twenty years at least, emerged. The younger man greeted her with a nod and a pinched smile, as though he was looking for any excuse to get out of there. On his arm, a cheerful redhead in her early thirties was unable to keep her eyes focused on one thing for more than a second before taking in another sight around her. She clapped as she made eye contact with Thandie.

"Check-in is right around the corner." Thandie pointed as she bent to help an older man out of the passenger seat of the next vehicle. "You must be Buzz," she said.

She only recognized this man as Buzz from his bio. The retired wrestler was one of the first Black men to win a paralympic gold medal in the sport. She could still make out his once-firm muscular frame beneath the white polo shirt with an American flag embroidered on the left chest.

"Thank you, dear. I never can navigate this whole getttin' in and gettin' out of the car with this incensing stick that everyone insists I use."

"Your doctor said he would only approve this trip if you promised to use it," said a middle-aged woman with light brown skin like Thandie's from the driver's side door.

"You must be Frances, Buzz's daughter. You can both head inside and check in. Just around the corner."

A rowdy group of sixty-somethings spilled out of a small taxi. Lightweight scarves covered in pastel floral motifs, strands of pearls the size of marbles, and more hairspray than was probably legal decorated each of the three women. *This will be a fun group*, Thandie thought and greeted them, showing them the way inside.

Two more cars pulled in. A good looking man emerged from one. His head tilted down and his eyes shifted around the lot as though he was looking for something. From the other car, a pretty woman, wearing a long, brown peasant skirt and tan blazer, peeked over the top of the vehicle. The man and woman nodded to each other, and the woman gave a little wave with a smile like they knew each other. Curious that they arrived in separate vehicles, Thandie began to approach, but as the pair came around the front of their cars, she felt like she was intruding into a private moment between the two.

Bowing out, Thandie headed inside where the other guests were lined up at check-in. America was playing hostess from her position beside the refreshments table. She was explaining the amenities of the barn to the taller woman and her friend.

Spotting a dropped wallet on the floor behind the young couple, Thandie picked up the black leather trifold and handed it to the man. She joined America but didn't want to interrupt the conversation.

"And that's when she told me about this place. I didn't even hesitate and booked right away," the tall one said.

America, with her hand to her chest, nodded. "I'm flattered that my article had such an impact on you. I do hope you will enjoy your stay this week. This is Thandie. She is the activities director and will be your guide for the next six days."

Thandie shook the ladies' hands. "It's a pleasure."

"I'm Margret, and this is Anne," the tall woman said in a fine British accent.

"So, Thandie, what do you have in store for us for the next

few days? I can't wait to feel well and rested," Anne, the shorter one, who was definitely from the American Midwest, said.

America put her arm in front of Thandie a little, like a defensive move, and spoke first. "So many great things planned. We wouldn't want to give it all away now. This way you can—"

"Enjoy each activity fully. Live in the moment, I always say." Thandie finished.

"Quite right," Margret agreed.

"I'll be making an announcement in a few minutes after all the guests are checked in," Thandie said and mouthed a thank you to America for saving her from having to explain the whole week's activities, which she was still uncertain about.

Thandie mingled with the guests, put faces to names, and made certain they were each getting off to a good start at The Foundry. Leo had everyone squared away in a few short minutes. He handed them each the keys to their cabin, and a map of the grounds—her idea. When everyone had gotten some food, she stood on a box near the *cucina* sign.

"Welcome to The Foundry Retreat," she said and waited until all eyes were trained on her. "My name is Thandie and I'm the activities director here. I hope you all had a good trip into town and we, here at the resort, are thrilled to have you for our inaugural wellness week." She got down from the box and walked amongst the tables. "This week, you will be challenged to look within and find peace, health, and freedom throughout the various activities. I encourage you to try everything, have an open mind, and certainly have fun. If you have any questions or concerns, just let me know.

"Now, for today, let's hit the ground, literally, with a nice, easy hike. In half an hour, we will meet back here and begin our first event. Wear some good hiking shoes or sneakers. Everything else you need for this, and all the events, will be provided. You can find out more each morning at the activities desk right over there, and I will also make an announcement each night at supper. Any questions?"

Three hands went up from the three rowdy friends. They huddled as far from Thandie as they could be while still being in the dining area. "Do we have to?" one said, and the others agreed.

"Of course not," Thandie said. "This is your vacation, after all. We meet back here in thirty minutes if you'd like to take part."

CHAPTER 8

The hike was a little more difficult the second time around that day, but the company was better. Thandie had waited in the barn as long as she could for the last straggler who had yet to check in, but there was only so much distracting she could do to keep the guests entertained and not focused on the delay.

She had passed out the hats, the canteens full of fresh water, and the walking sticks, and showed the guests the trail route on the map. But alas, they had to go. Even Buzz joined the hike, which made Thandie glad.

Standing near the top of the hill with the overlook just ahead was the ideal spot to keep an eye on the guests that had gone up. Margret, having taken the lead with two of the other couples in tow, took photos and selfies. The trio of sixty-somethings had not joined the activity, as she had suspected after their interaction during the check-in announcements.

Down below, at the old dock, she could make out Buzz and his daughter pointing out into the emptied lake. Though the view was nice from the dock, the scenery from where she stood lit her imagination on fire. With the wide flower-filled plain, yellows and whites dancing in the sun, and bright red tufts of long grasses swaying in the breeze, she could see all the ways it called to be tamed and nurtured. The natural garden was a stunning backdrop for photos or even painting. *An artist retreat would be a big hit*, she thought.

From the corner of her vision, the guests at the perch gathered their packs and walking sticks. She checked downhill to see if any newly arrived guests were joining them on the hike. But no one new was visible. They weren't in a hurry, and she wanted the guests to not feel rushed through their experience. They had six full days of adventures to make it through. Pacing the events was a top priority.

"You ready to head back down?" Thandie asked. "Watch your step. The ground here is really dry and loose."

The man whom she had assumed wouldn't enjoy this activity based on his preference sheet and the particular line that told *walking was okay if he had to*, sported the widest smile of the group. "What a nice little hike," he said and shook her hand when he approached.

Thandie now knew him to be Brent, the one who had arrived with the overly perky redhead, Daisy. She appeared from behind him as though conjured by the mere thought of her, and she rested her chin on Brent's shoulder.

"What's the story with all the docks, though? Was this some sort of lake or something?" Daisy asked.

Thandie was glad that America had gotten her up to speed on the history of the area. She answered confidently, "You got it right, Daisy. This used to be a lake, and the section over there"— she pointed at the retreat area and the small town just over the hill in the distance—"that's Christmas Cove. Though it used to be its own town, the Cove is now part of Elizabethtown, which is where you came in today."

"That's where we came in, too, on the train," the shorter woman, Anne, said.

The small group gathered and listened intently to her

explanation. "When the dam blew out downstream of here, wildflowers and grasses took over the fertile lakebed," Thandie said as she looked at the scenery. "A beautiful accident, don't you think?"

"Quite right," Margret said.

"I just love a good British accent," Daisy said. "What part of the ol' isles are you from, anyway?"

"Oh, dear. We don't call it *the isles*. I hail from Lincolnshire. Best plum loaf in the world and the prettiest flowers you'll find anywhere. Though this is a lovely view, don't misunderstand me."

"I would never," Thandie jested.

"I hear a bit of an accent in you as well. Let me guess. Boer by way of the Midwest?" Margret asked.

Shocked at the woman's accuracy, Thandie smiled. "That's incredible, though I'm not whole Boer. My mother came from a Dutch plantation family that had been on that land for a century or more, but she fell in love and married my father, who is a native South African. She was disowned by my grandparents, and he had nothing more to offer my mother there. So, they moved to America before I was born. And the rest is history, they say." They began the descent back to the retreat. "How did you do that, anyway?"

"I have a knack for languages and dialects. It's a hobby, really. Plus, I view a lot of foreign tele on my various travels."

"She's a nosy nelly, that's what she is," her friend, Anne, said with a distinctly American accent.

"My parents never talked about it more than that, and they settled in Iowa. Farming was something they were both good at, so it was a natural occupation."

"Hence the Midwest influence," Margret added.

The other man piped in. "What about me? Can you tell where I'm from?" his eyebrows pulsed upwards on his wrinkled forehead.

"Florida. Central," Margret said without missing a beat.

"Well, I'll be!" he said. "That's a talent like none other. I'm William." He shook her hand.

"Margret," she said. "And this is my best friend, Anne. Pleasure to meet you."

The small group walked ahead while continuing their conversation. Thandie made good use of the high vantage point and took her phone from her cross-body bag. She snapped a few shots of the wildflowers and flipped the camera around for a selfie or two. Picking her best angle, she messaged a photo to JB, who would appreciate the tiny update.

As she zipped her bag, the phone buzzed and vibrated. Glad to have a signal for once, she looked. Only, it wasn't a message back from JB that had buzzed, it was a voicemail. From Davis.

Her heart pounded in her chest. She sucked in breath and held it while she decided what to do. Until yesterday, he hadn't so much as called her, texted her, or anything. Not even a random midnight drop in her DMs for months. She was fairly certain that she had said everything she needed to say to him before hanging up on him in the car. *So, what could he possibly need now?*

Turning off her phone, she put it away in her bag. She had waited months to know what had spooked him out of their wedding, and now he could wait on her to listen to his silly message. With her walking stick in hand, she began down the hill only to stop in her tracks a few steps later and dig her phone back out from the bag.

Patience wasn't her strongest trait. She scrambled to get the thing out, but her eyes shifted from her bag to a man on a bike barreling down the path right in her direction. The front tire looked to have come off the rim and was flapping back and forth on the frame.

"Stop, stop," she yelled, though the man had likely tried that already.

"Get out of the way. Whoa, WHOA!" he shouted as he skidded toward her on the narrow trail.

Hitting an exposed root, he tumbled off the bike and took her legs out from under her as he went one way, and the bike flew the other. He took hold of her with his arms wrapped around her body and protected her as they rolled to a stop at the level area several feet down from where the incursion had begun.

"Are you alright?" he said and cradled her head in his hand.

His body was half on top of her, with the majority of his weight on the ground. As he picked some grass and a twig out of her hair, his blue eyes twinkled and reflected the cornflower blue sky back at her. She swallowed hard at her body's reaction to this stranger. As he continued to inspect her for injuries, she lay there in shock, but noticed his soft grin and concerned pinch of his brow.

Thandie sat up. "I think I'm okay. But are you?" She looked him over and flicked some dirt from his shoulder.

"I am so sorry." He stood and reached down for her hand. "Mortified doesn't cover it."

"It's not your fault. The bicycle tire did you wrong," Thandie joked and faced the man. Her hand rested in his, and his fingers wrapped around to the back of her wrist. "Oh, my gosh. You're bleeding. Let me help you."

"You have a survival kit or something?" he joked, though embarrassment was evident in his eyeroll.

Turning his hand over, blood beaded up and dripped from a cut on his forearm. Without even thinking, she dug in her bag for the first aid kit. It was small, but held bandages, antibiotic ointment, and alcohol wipes. She took the wipe packet in her teeth and tore the paper open. With her free hand, she took the soaked pad and lingered over the wound. "This is going to sting."

"Just do it," he said and looked away.

Thandie cleaned the cut, with only a single breath sucked in through the man's teeth. Using her teeth again, she opened the ointment packet and spread the clear goo over the cut. "Almost done," she said. "You can look, you know."

His eyes were closed tightly, and he shook his head back and forth like a little boy.

"There, there," she said as she blew cold air on the exposed skin in order to dry it before sticking the bandage in place. "All done. You can open your eyes now."

He turned his face back in her direction and released the breath that she wondered if he had been holding that whole time. She stifled a giggle and cleaned up the mess.

"Thank you for this," he said with all sincerity.

"You're very welcome. Just doing my job," Thandie said. She shoved the trash inside a small plastic baggy and placed it back in her bag. "Oh no. Oh no. Oh no." Panic seized her chest, and she began searching the ground near where they had come to a stop.

"What is it?" he said and looked with her. "What exactly are we looking for?"

"My phone," she said. "It was in my hand when you crashed into me. I need it."

"It's only a phone, you can get another," he said. "I'll replace it if that's alright with you?"

"No," she screamed too firmly. "You don't understand. I need to find it now." Urgency cracked her voice, and she scanned the hillside up to where they first collided.

"I'm sure it's not far. Let's search in a grid," he suggested logically. "That way we won't miss it."

Organized, she thought. They each took a side of the trail and walked up the hill in step with one another. She never wanted to listen to a voicemail more than she did at that very moment. Whatever Davis had to say, she wanted to know. She had a fiery need to know. Even if all he said was that she was the worst. Not knowing was crueler than whatever he had to say to her, and her imagination was already running away with the narrative.

"What's so important?" the man asked. "Oh, wait. I think I see it over there."

Thandie followed the line of his pointed finger straight to a muddy puddle a yard off the trail. The phone stuck halfway out of the mud and the screen blinked on and off as though it was shorting out.

"Fantastic," she said and pushed some brush aside.

The phone was sopping wet with gritty mud and was making some sort of noise that reminded her of a coyote's cry. She flung the muck from the screen and wiped the rest on her pants leg, but the device came away muddier than before she had attempted cleaning it. That was the moment when she realized she was covered head to toe in the same mud.

Looking at the man, she saw that he was covered too, and the absurdity of the situation overtook her sensibilities. Laughing was all that remained to do. She pointed at the man and, seeing the mud all over himself too, joined her revelry.

"Aren't we a pair!" he chuckled.

"Come on, I know somewhere we can get cleaned up." She pointed down the trail. "Where were you heading anyway?"

"The Foundry Retreat," he said and picked up the broken bicycle from the side of the trail. "Do you know it?"

She realized the blue bike looked just like the one she had back at camp. "Are you one of the guests there?"

"Sure am," he said. "I'm Grant. I figure we should be introduced since I about killed you, and you tended to my booboo."

"Thandie," she said as they took it easy down the slick slope.

In her mind, she ran through the preference sheets and guest info that she remembered from the binder. Grant was the last guest who hadn't checked in yet when the hike began.

"Are you staying at the resort too?" he asked.

She nodded but something stopped her from saying more.

"I'm checking the place out this week," he said. "It's new, you know?"

Could this be the spy sent by the investor? Her money was on Brent and Daisy at the moment, but she couldn't rule out a guy, alone, at a wellness retreat. Although, it was almost too obvious to be believable.

"It seems nice so far," she said. "Don't you think?"

He took her hand for a moment and helped her down a steep section where more roots had been exposed from erosion. Apparently, she hadn't taken that close a look when scouting it out in the first place. Between the roots and loose gravel cover, the plant species invading the worn path, and the afternoon sun beating down on them, she noted that the hike should be saved for a morning or a cloudy day instead.

"I'll have to give my opinion about the bike maintenance," he joked. "I'm sure the owner wouldn't want to be sued for something like this. I wonder if they have liability?"

"I'm sure you can overlook this one. I mean, just think if the tire hadn't blown, you wouldn't have run me over. Maybe I should find out if *you* have liability?" She raised an eyebrow at him, and he chuckled.

"Right!" he said and flexed his fingers around her hand. "I'll let this one slide."

His unintentional pun made her snort. Thandie covered her mouth with the back of her hand that was holding the walking stick.

"Watch out with that thing," he said. The sudden jerk to cover her mouth caused the stick to swing upward towards his chin and nearly slice his face.

She dropped the hiking stick. "We are quite a pair, as you pointed out."

They laughed and joked all the way back to the barn where a cross-looking Leo stood at the doors waiting for them. Waiting for her.

"Mr. Goldie, I see you found our activities director on the trail," Leo said.

Grant dragged the broken bike to the covered bicycle parking area and let it fall in a heap beside the neatly parked others. "The bike broke," Grant said.

Thandie stood in front of him. "You knew who I was the whole time?"

He shrugged and turned his attention back to Leo. "Leo told me to find you. I was to ride up the hill and spot a woman wearing a baseball cap, tan cargo pants, and a white top. I couldn't miss you. And I didn't!" He chuckled. "Great hike though. I look forward to the next activity." Grant flicked some mud from his shirt. "After I get cleaned up."

Thandie buried her head in her hands, shaking it, as his footsteps scuffed the ground walking away from her.

"Director?" Leo said and motioned for her to follow him around the side of the barn.

"I'm so sorry, Leo. His bike failed and he ran me over. We ended up in the mud and I had no idea he was a guest. He got a cut on his arm, and other than being filthy, we are both ok."

"I know this is your first day, but we have to do better than this since we don't know which one of them is here on behalf of the investor."

"Oh," she said and bit her grinning lip. "I know."

"You do? How?"

"It's them." She pointed over her shoulder. "Brent and Daisy. He was very interested in the lake and asked a bunch of questions."

"Are you certain?" Leo said and kicked the gravel beneath his feet.

"Pretty sure, but I can find out."

"No. I mean, you can't ask. But what you *can* do is give them, all of them, your full attention. Show them the best we have to offer," Leo said. "Do you think you can do that? If you're correct, that makes it all the more real."

"I will do my job. Well."

Leo took a calming breath and centered on her gaze. "We got this, right?"

"Yes. I'm not worried," she assured and high-fived Leo.

"That makes one of us. Anyway, are you alright? You look worse for wear."

"I'm fine." She took her phone from her pocket. "But this didn't fare too well."

Leo took the phone. "It's not like we get a good signal in these parts anyway. I can take a look if you'd like."

"Please do. I'm going to go get cleaned up," Thandie said and turned. "Supper's in an hour."

CHAPTER 9

Grant redressed the cut on his arm after cleaning up from his tumble in the mud with The Foundry's gorgeous activities director, though he shouldn't have noticed her in that way. Thandie had done a superior job, even while covered in dirt and having just been run over by him. The wound appeared less swollen after his shower, but stung like an open paper cut whenever he moved his wrist. He hoped the cut wouldn't preclude him from participating in any of the week's planned events.

Grant had only been there for a few hours and hadn't made the best impression. Nor had the retreat for that matter. First, the place seemed understaffed. The owner, Leo had greeted him and checked him in, while Thandie, the only person working in activities, was already on a hike with the other guests. Secondly, the bicycle had broken on his first day. Although, he admitted, he might have taken the bike on a rather rocky off-trail adventure, complete with a hard landing from jumping over a fallen tree trunk. The landing may have bent the rim and flattened the tire, which might have led to its ill-fated demise.

Due to his own reckless actions, he couldn't hold the

equipment situation against the retreat, and he couldn't fault them for being understaffed. All of his needs had been thusly met so far. And, as he looked at the fluffy white bedding and copious amounts of pillows arranged on the bed that he couldn't wait to flop into later, it was evident that everything had been thought of, short-staffing aside.

Scoping out the other cabins as he had walked down to his, he noted that his was the tiniest. Even though the others looked bigger, the square room was all the space he needed. On the right side beside the front door, a U-shaped kitchenette with barstools on the peninsula separated the room. A washroom was tucked away behind the kitchen next to a narrow closet, and the bed was positioned between two windows to the left side of the studio space. The rich dark wood slats looked to be original to the structure, the chinking still visible from inside and out, though it looked and smelled like it had recently been oiled.

He ran his hands along one of the hewn logs like a kid in a school hallway, feeling the texture and tiny imperfections of the surface. He felt instantly connected with the space, with this little plot of land that someone had once loved, and now had a new purpose.

The room was serene, and even a bell ringing out from beyond the trees surrounding his cabin didn't disturb the atmosphere. *The barn*, he guessed. Announcing the dinner service was a nice touch, and he hoped all the meals would be declared in such a way. It provided a quality of romanticism to the day. The bell, low and thick, resonated a calm throughout the countryside and into his small space. At the same time, a group of three birds, perched on the whitewashed windowsill, chirped outside the glass and turned their heads towards the ringing.

Outside, his log-style cabin had white painted trim and doorjambs. Black flower boxes hung at the two windows beside the front door and held vines of small yellow flowers that spilled out over the sides as though reaching for the ground.

He took the long way around to the barn and investigated the property from a different vantage point. The cabins ranged in size from multi-room, two-story houses to his tiny, one room, hunting-style cabin. Some exteriors were of gray washed shingles, others were traditional log-style cabins, and one Victorian cottage with light blue paint and copper accents caught his eye.

All the cabins looked well-kept and safe. This wasn't like a typical hotel where all the rooms are similar in their layout and design. These were all completely different, and Grant planned on befriending some of the other guests to get the inside scoop of their accommodations. Meanwhile, he would need to focus on what he could see with his own eyes.

In the distance, his eyes saw something statuesque and glowing like amber standing outside the barn doors. Thandie. She was going to be trouble for him. He could feel it, just like he had felt her fitting in his arms as they tumbled to a stop on the trail. Trouble aside, it wouldn't hurt him to make friends with the person that was most likely to help him to get a sense of the resort on a more personal level. Though he had to be cognizant of his rule: No getting close to people on these kinds of scouting trips. It only complicated his ability to give a thorough and honest assessment.

His initial assessment, as he approached the barn, was that she was wonderful.

Thandie held open one of the heavy glass-and-steel barn doors and greeted the guests for dinner. She must have seen him coming. With her hand extended over her head, she waved it wildly back and forth like she was signaling a spacecraft. He had to admire her enthusiasm to make him feel welcome.

Though he looked to be the last to come up for dinner, she remained outside, waiting for him to make his way. Knowing that someone, anyone, was waiting on him for any reason, grated against his nature. He was impatient and knew the value of someone's time. He didn't want to waste hers, as much as he didn't want his own abused.

But instead of speeding up, which his brain was urging him to do, he kept a steady gait and used the interlude to admire the scenery. At the center of his field of vision, a halo of reflected sunlight surrounded Thandie and crowned her with lazy pink and orange clouds in the sky beyond. A smile stretched across the whitest teeth and rosiest lips Grant had ever seen, and her skin glowed golden brown from the setting sun.

There was something cat-like about her appearance. Her blue, almond-shaped eyes slanted up at the outside corners and long, dark lashes elegantly framed her features. Her small nose came to a delicate point and her dark brunette hair framed and shadowed her cheekbones in a way that made him want to brush the springy waves behind her ear.

Thandie was a most unique beauty. If she were taller, she might have been a high-fashion model. She was definitely of mixed-race heritage. *Maybe Caribbean?* he wondered. He was as Caucasian as one could get. He looked down at his exposed forearms and thought perhaps he'd find some time during his stay to get some sun.

Feeling self-conscious was not a sensation Grant was accustomed to, like knowing there were spiders crawling all over his skin, he squirmed inside. He waved and turned around, fully prepared to head back to his cabin and eat granola for dinner instead of facing the woman that had no idea how nervous she made him. He had a rule: Don't get involved. More than that, he had a heart that he had closed and locked the door to years ago, and he had no intention of ever finding the key for it again.

"Wait," she yelled and ran after him. "Grant, right? Where are you going? You know it's suppertime. Everyone else is already in the *cucina*. Don't you want to join?"

He was pinned down and had no excuse but to go with her. "I

thought I forgot something back in my room, but it can wait." He lied.

"If it's important, I can go with you for some company," Thandie said and tilted her head ever so slightly so that her hair fell away and exposed her long neck. "If you want."

"It's fine. Really." Because he was lying. "It can wait." Because it was nothing more than cowardice.

"If you're sure," she said.

"Thandie," he said and took a deep breath. "I'm really sorry about running you over earlier."

"It's fine—"

"It's not," he interrupted. "But I'm so ashamed of letting you think I didn't know you worked here, and that I am a guest. It was poor form of me."

"Grant," she said his name like a question. "You're forgiven. Now can we go in and eat?"

"Yes, actually. I'm starving, and I'm dying to see what the chef has to offer. Mr. Thorpe raved about this *cucina* when I checked in."

Grant held the door open and led Thandie through with his hand resting on the small of her back. She glanced over her shoulder. A hint of a grin pulled her cheek up. But the door slammed with a gust of wind like a warning to him. Like a reminder that he didn't know this woman, nor was he there for some sort of speed dating vacation.

Grant had a job to do. Thandie was nothing more than a beautiful distraction. The truth was, he may have locked the door to his heart, but his body hadn't gotten the memo. His chest flexed, and he drew his hand away from her back.

"You can sit wherever you'd like. Supper will be served soon." Thandie motioned to an empty seat beside a tall woman. "But you might want to sit with Margret and her friend, Anne. They won't bite."

Grant sat down at the small square table and greeted the two ladies sitting beside him. Small talk was one of his least favorite forms of communication, but one that he had become a pro at in practice. His consulting services and constant relocations meant that he often engaged in mindless talk with people he neither cared for nor would likely see again. This was no exception. He would be gone in a few days, and they would never think of him again.

Pleasant, friendly, boring, that was his modus.

Being the unremarkable-yet-amiable sleuth could work on everyone else, but he'd already shown his true colors to one person. In his vulnerable moment, covered in mud, laying nearly on top of a perfect stranger, and bleeding on her, she had seen him. She might not have even realized it in the chaos that she had glimpsed his weakness. Her.

CHAPTER 10

Out of Grant's periphery, Thandie moved through the space, greeting guests, pouring water, and lighting up the room like a firefly at twilight. She spotted him looking at her, and he turned his head quickly back to the conversation. Thinking that wasn't right, he looked back to her and gave a low wave which also didn't feel right. His body was making a fool out of him.

She bobbed and weaved around the tables on her way towards him. "Everything alright over here?" she asked the whole table, though he could tell she was really just asking him. "I thought it looked like one of you waved me over?" She poured water into his glass and topped off the others. "Supper should be out any moment. It's self-serve at the sideboard."

"What's on the menu?" Anne asked to his left.

Thandie pinched her brows together and looked up as though the answer might be on the ceiling. "You know, I'm not certain. Do you want me to go check with the chef?"

"That won't be necessary," Margret said. "Ignore my friend here. She'll eat whatever it is."

"I know the chef has planned according to the preference sheets that each of you filed before check-in."

"Do you think the chef will come out and explain the dishes like they do on those fancy food shows?" Anne asked.

Thandie looked back at the *cucina* and then placed her hands on her hips. "Would you look at that? How did the chef put all that food out without any of us seeing? Since I've been here, I haven't actually met the chef, to be honest with you. I'm just as curious to know him as you are."

"You haven't met the chef?" Grant asked. "Shouldn't you know who's doing all the cooking?"

"All I know is that all my meals here so far have been perfect. No complaints from me." She took the nearly empty pitcher and tapped her painted, pink fingernails on the bottom, causing it to play a little musical trill. "I'm going to go fill this up and see if I can coax the chef out for a meet and greet."

No sooner had Thandie walked away than a white-hatted and cloaked young man came through a side door opposite the *cucina*. His black hair poked out from the rim of his hat, his face had a warm healthy tan, and his deep brown eyes reminded Grant of his trip to Greece last year.

The chef cleared his throat and announced dinner was served. "I prepare for you tonight, a selection based on your *preferenza*." The chef's Italian accent was thick and smooth like honey. "Though the—how you say, *pietanze*? The dishes, the entrées, may not be what you envision, I hope you like very much. *Mangia!*" he said and bowed with his hand over his heart. "Enjoy."

"Definitely Italian," Margret said and stood from the table. "But there's something else. I'll have to think on it. Greek—no, French . . ." Her voice trailed off as she moved away.

Grant leaned over to the woman on his left, who was still seated. "What's that about?"

"Mags fancies herself a linguist of sorts, but she's just nosy is all. I'm Anne," she said. Her smile cut a jolly line across her round face and wrinkled the skin around her eyes.

"Grant. Pleasure to meet you," he said and took her hand, helping her to her feet.

The other guests queued at the buffet and were busy heaping their plates with the assorted fare. Despite fatigue pushing at his eyelids, Grant knew he needed to try all the food. He covered a small yawn with the back of his hand. Travel days weren't his favorite by a long shot.

Margret returned to the table first and placed her plate down. "You're not eating?"

"Not yet," he said. "I'll let everyone else go through first."

"A gentleman," she said and sat down. "What brings a nice-looking bloke like you to a wellness retreat all alone?"

"How do you know I'm alone?" he said.

"Because if you were my man, I would dare not let you go anywhere without me." She hid a giggle behind a fork full of tomato and basil salad. "You're single?"

He nodded at the woman's uncanny ability to parse things out for herself. "Is it that obvious?"

"Yes. So, answer my question. What brings you out here?"

"I, um . . ." *Usually had a canned answer ready to go.* "Work." It wasn't a lie, though he was certain she would ask more questions. He beat her to the inevitable. "I needed a break from the day-to-day grind. This place seemed like a good way to do that."

"And what is the grind?" she asked as Anne returned to the table with a modest dinner sampling on her plate.

"I'm a consultant," he said, knowing it was easier to weave as much truth into his ruse as possible than risk getting caught in a lie. "It's a good job. I get to travel a lot."

"Oh," Anne said between bites of thinly sliced beef that dripped with gravy. "We love to travel. That's all we do now that we are both widows and retired."

"I'm sorry to hear that," he said, and he was. "It's difficult to lose someone you love."

"Speaking from experience?"

He pinched his lips tightly and nodded as the image flashed in his mind of the woman he had loved once. She had taken the key to his heart with her to the grave. At risk of feeling emotions that he had been avoiding for longer than he could admit, he stood from the table. "I think I'll get some food now."

Anne placed a hand on his shoulder the way people do when they truly understand the deep hurt hiding under the surface. He appreciated the gesture and didn't know why now, after nearly ten years, he had chosen that moment to call up his wife's memory. The pain that he had so expertly disguised beneath the mask of an international corporate consultant with no time for love or fancy was surfacing with force.

He blinked away the moisture fogging his eyes and bowed out of the lady's presence. At the buffet, Grant looked at the food, though he was seeing past it. He mindlessly picked and spooned each item onto a plate, numb to his appetite.

"It's the darnedest thing," Thandie said as she bumped shoulders with him, tearing him from his solitary contemplation. "I went to talk to the chef, and no one was in there."

"What? What did you say?" Grant said as her words sunk in. "Oh, the chef was out here. You didn't see him introduce dinner?"

Thandie looked over her shoulder into the dining area as though she was wanting to spot the chef. "I just don't get it. It's as though he, I'm pretty sure he is a he, I barely saw him through a curtain of fettuccine yesterday—"

"He. And we think he's Italian."

"We?"

"Margret. She's some sort of linguist, and she thinks he's Italian."

"I hear she's just nosey," Thandie whispered as she filled her own plate. "But don't tell anyone I said that."

Grant pinched his lips and mimed turning a lock. Her laugh was the sweetest reprieve from his depressive reverie about his loss. "Your clandestine gossiping is safe with me."

"Thank you," she said and scooped the tomato and basil salad onto her plate. "This is the strangest collection of food I think I've ever seen. There's Mediterranean, sushi, and whatever that is, and this—" She held up something on a skewer that looked like a banana dipped in barbeque sauce and sprinkled with chopped cauliflower. "What is this?"

Grant pointed at the table. "That is squid-ink risotto, and that is broccoli rabe. This," he held up the skewer, "is corn on the cob. Though I've never seen it prepared this way."

Thandie stopped all movement but her eyes. Astonishment stretched her face, and her eyes were wide. She put the skewered corn back on the tray. "I hate corn on the cob. If I never see another ear of corn again, I'd be perfectly happy."

"Now that you mention it, I don't like octopus, and there it is."

"How do you know what all these things are? Are you a chef too?" Thandie asked him.

This time, Grant laughed so loud that the room quieted, and the guests turned their attention to him. He addressed the group and waved them off as his laugh subsided.

"What is so funny?" Thandie asked. Her hand went to her hip, and he could see heat rise in her cheeks.

He merely pointed at the buffet. Little chalk board signs sat in front of each item and described the menu. "I can read."

Thandie grunted, and Grant realized he might have teased her too far, given their rocky start on the hiking trail.

"I honestly didn't even notice the little signs. I suppose I was just so hungry, not to mention puzzled by the vanishing chef, that I was mindlessly filling my plate."

"I know the feeling." Grant looked at his own plate and then to her nearly identical one with one of each item neatly arranged around the rim. "Do you want to sit with us? There's an empty seat."

Thandie looked around him at the table where Margret and

Anne were sitting, and back at him. "Sit with the cool kids? On the first day?" A grin. A giggle.

Her laugh was like a song, and Grant felt a crack forming in the wall around his heart in that moment. He would very much like to tease her back, and he was glad that he had a whole week to try. She followed him around the maze of little tables, and he directed her around his side with his free arm.

"Mind if I join you?" Thandie asked the ladies, who quickly agreed. "Grant was just telling me how much he loves octopus. Did you try some?"

"It's delicious," Anne said and took a long, slimy piece. "I've never had it prepared like this. But Grant, it doesn't look like you put any on your plate."

He shook his head at Thandie. "She's mistaken. I do not like octopus. And she doesn't like corn."

"Funny," Margret said and pushed the black risotto off to the side of her plate. "I don't like squid ink, and yet here it is. Anne, is there something the chef prepared that you don't prefer too?"

Anne inspected her plate and then looked over to the buffet. "As a matter of fact. I had put down that I don't like creamed vegetables. And there was that broccoli dish, though I've never seen broccoli like that before."

Grant was catching on, but didn't know if he should say anything. It appeared that the chef had created dinner based on their preference sheets, but had used their dislikes instead of their likes. He was curious whether the decision had been a mistake or if the chef had intentionally prepared the disliked dishes in a new way. The chef had even encouraged the group to give things a try. If it was an intentional act, Grant was impressed by the chef's audacity and would certainly include it in his report. He hoped for Leo's sake that the chef hadn't made a huge miscalculation, though.

"Do you think I should go ask?" Thandie said and was already getting up from the table.

Grant intercepted her hand and tugged ever so slightly, causing her to pause. He pulled a little harder, and she sat back down. Their hands stayed together long after the need was there for him to touch her. It was as though the whole world was silent for a split second and then rushed back at him all at once. Touching her was like a tide going out only to be followed by a tsunami wave of butterflies and heartbeats.

He snapped back his hand. The shock on her face was surely mimicked on his own, though neither of them said a word.

"Single, huh?" Margret teased and broke the air surrounding them.

"I think I'll go find the chef now," Thandie said, and this time, got up on the far side of her chair so as to avoid his touch again.

After she walked away, Grant eyed Margret. "Look what you did. Made her leave," he said.

"I wouldn't be so sure. Just you wait and see. I think she likes you," Margret said with a single nod that proclaimed that was that.

Anne leaned over to him. "See. Nosey."

"I heard that," Margret said and turned up her chin. Straightening her back, she cleared her throat and motioned with her eyes as a warning. And not a moment too soon. "What did you find out about this meal, dear?"

Thandie's hip brushed against Grant's upper-arm as she came back around to her seat, and he instinctively looked. It was only a split second. But he *had* looked.

"Chef wasn't there," Thandie said. "But mark my words, I will uncover the truth about this intriguing meal." Thandie took a bite of the octopus. "You're right, Anne. This is really good." Grant sucked in a chuckle as she skewered the remaining pieces with her fork and filled her cheeks to the breaking point.

"Maybe you should try that corn after all," Grant joked.

"Not in your lifetime."

"You can't give up corn forever, you know."

"I can try," Thandie laughed and took a bite of something else, savoring the flavors with a gentle grin.

As Grant skewered his own piece of octopus, Leo came around Thandie's back. He leaned over her shoulder and spoke into her ear. Grant tilted his body to hear, to eavesdrop, but was unable to make out any words. Thandie nodded as though she understood what was being told to her.

When Leo was done, he stood and nodded to them. "Enjoying dinner?"

"Yes, very much," Margret said.

"Delicious," Anne added.

"Compliments to the chef," Grant said. As Leo turned away, he leaned over to Thandie. "Everything alright?"

She shook her head and forced a smile. "Please excuse me for a moment." Thandie got up from her seat and placed her napkin on her plate like she was finished. He watched her walk across the room, pull a chair towards the wall and step up onto the seat.

As she clapped her hands, the dozen guests stopped what they were doing, mid chew, mid cackle, mid thought, and turned towards the sound. The tension in her face radiated bad news. She took a deep breath. Her chest filled slowly, and he could see she was holding the air in for a few seconds before letting it out. He was on the edge of his seat.

She began. "Good evening to each of you. I'm happy to officially welcome you to The Foundry Retreat and begin our week together. For those of you who don't remember names well, my name is Thandie and I'm the activities director here." Leo returned and handed her a stack of papers. "I have the tentative schedule for the week." She stepped down quickly and passed the papers to the closest guest. "Will you pass these around? Thank you." Returning to her perch, she continued. "There is one caveat I must correct. The bonfire, listed for tonight, has been rescheduled for Wednesday evening due to the rainy weather."

And there it was, the bad news. The first evening's event was rained out. Soft murmurs livened the room.

She continued. "You can't have a fire in the rain." She paused as though waiting for a laugh. When none came, she swallowed and tucked a curly strand behind her ear. "I've placed a basket beside the front door with ponchos and umbrellas. These items are supplied for your use during your stay, and I only ask that you return them, or leave them in your cabin when it's time to say goodbye."

"Is it gonna rain all week?" a young lady asked in a melodic southern accent.

"I'm sorry, the weather here is a little unpredictable, so I can't say for sure, but it looks like it will be fine. Just your typical late spring showers. In the meantime, as this is your first evening here, I suggest rest and hydration. We'll see you bright and early in here for breakfast. At nine-thirty, I will meet you in the gazebo for yoga."

CHAPTER 11

The rain squall had been short, and other than canceling the bonfire, it hadn't caused more glitches in Thandie's schedule. In the morning, clear skies and bright sun energized her for the day's activities, which she got straight to work on setting up. She was glad to have a bicycle handy for getting herself around the property. It was, however, not so useful when it came to transporting equipment from the barn to anywhere else. By her third trip back and forth to the gazebo, with yoga mats balanced on her knees and slung over her shoulders, Thandie knew she needed another way.

She parked the bike and walked around the back side of the barn, where she recalled seeing an old woodshed. Its three walls held up a slanted roof ideal for rain or snow to fall from. Under the roof, she found scrap metal, chunks of planks and wood, orange wiring that went to nowhere, and buckets, lots of empty buckets. "What a junkyard!" she said.

"Excuse me," a man called out. His voice was scruffy and worn from his many years.

Thandie whirled around and put a hand over her racing heart. "You gave me a fright. I didn't see you there," she said.

"Sorry, I didn't mean to scare you." The man held out his hand. "I'm Pa."

She shook the old man's dirt-covered hand, while in her mind she added to her running tally of how many times she had been covered with mud or dirt so far this week. "Nice to meet you," she said. "Leo and America told me about you. They said you're a man of many talents and that you could get me anything I need."

"Is that so?" Pa said as he wiped the mud from his hands after having shaken and dirtied hers. "I'll have to have a talk with them two. But since you're here, do you need any help?"

"No, that's alright. But I appreciate the offer. I'm just looking for something I can use to help get all the supplies over to the gazebo."

"I can rig something up for you really quick, if you'd like." Pa offered his assistance again.

Thandie knew she was perfectly capable of solving this particular problem on her own. Not only was she determined to show the owners that she could handle her job, but she also had something to prove to herself too. She didn't need a man to do for her what she could do alone.

"Am I free to use any of this stuff?" she asked.

Pa stepped back, having gotten wind of her independence. He smiled. "It's all yours. There's a cart over there, and all the tools and screws or bolts you might need are against that wall there. Don't hesitate to ask for help if you need it."

From his coaxing tone, he probably knew that she wouldn't ask. She didn't know him well enough to show any sign of weakness or helplessness. So she settled on a quick thank-you and began rummaging through the piles of junk.

Beneath bundles of sticks, she found a soft-sided red cart with four fat tires that looked ideal for avoiding getting stuck in the muddy ground around the gazebo.

With the cart's scraps unloaded, she walked back up front to where her bike was parked next to a pile of yoga mats and water bottles. Using some faded blue cordage that she picked from the junk heap, she lashed the long cart handle to the back mudguard. With the buggy now in tow, she loaded the items that were staged outside and, with plenty of extra space in the cart, went back inside the barn for the rest of the gear that she needed.

On her way through the lounge, she greeted Brent and Daisy, and Buzz and his daughter. They were enjoying a friendly conversation from their spots on the champagne velvet couches near the stone fireplace. The room had a stunning yet cozy feel. The fireplace bisected two sections of floor-to-ceiling windows with nothing but green trees visible through the glass on either side. She didn't want to interrupt, and made her way to the loft.

Upstairs in the office, Leo sat behind his desk and sat up straight when she entered. The old landline phone, with its curly cord, was pressed against his ear. He put a finger over his lips, telling her to be quiet.

She tiptoed to the bin labeled Yoga/Pilates and took the whole bin in hand. Tiptoeing back across the loft, Leo held up his hand for her to wait. As he finished wrapping up the conversation, she checked her watch. Forty-five minutes until the guests would begin arriving at the gazebo for the day's first activity.

"I look forward to seeing you later this week. Goodbye now," Leo said and hung up the phone. A smile pulled at one cheek. "That was good news. The investor wants to come here himself. I don't know if that means he doesn't trust his spy, or what. He said he's going to be in the city, and since he'll be within a couple hours of here, he wants to check it out."

"That's good news, I suppose. But what if this whole thing is a disaster?"

"*Is* this whole thing going to be a disaster, Thandie?" Leo said.

She shook her head, though inside, she was totally unsure.

"That's what I expected you to say. Is everything set for today?" he asked and scribbled some things on a yellow legal pad.

"I'm in a good rhythm today. Yoga is coming up in a little bit and"—she lifted the bin in front of her chest—"it's hard to carry all this stuff on a bike, so I rigged an old cart to the rear of mine. I hope that's alright."

He nodded while writing on his notepad.

"A golf cart would be a nice addition if we get the funding."

"I'll put it on the list." He chuckled without taking his eyes off the paper.

There's probably a million things on that list, she thought.

"I've got to get going," she said, not wanting to be rude.

"Of course, go on," Leo said.

Stepping back outside, the sun glimmered off the bike's shiny blue paint. The wheels were clean and free of the mud that had been covering the rims before she'd gone in for the last of the supplies. Pa stood behind the bike with a wide grin. He had come and attached the cart to the rear axle on one side and replaced the existing handle with a long, bent piece of steel. The mud had been washed off and the items in the cart stacked neatly.

"Well? Will this do?" he said. "I know you said you didn't need my help, but—"

What else could she say? "It's perfect." Walking forward, she placed the bin on the ground and took a closer look at the man's handiwork. "This is way better than what I came up with," she rightly admitted. Though her rig would have worked well enough, this one would perform much better in the long run.

"What you need is a golf cart," Pa said.

"It's on the list." She snickered.

"Have you seen his list?" Pa chuckled back. "Leo has one as long as his arm. All I'm saying is, don't hold your breath waiting for it."

"Thank you very much for this. I mean it."

Pa stood at attention and saluted. "Happy to be of service."

Thandie mirrored his posture. "Dismissed," she said as she played along with Pa.

As he walked away, she loaded the additional supplies into the cart. Getting atop the bike was slightly more interesting with the extra load on the back, but the trip back to the gazebo was so much easier than her previous journeys had been.

Easier, that was, until her rear wheel sank into a patch of soft soil, causing the bike to stop and topple over.

She was sure a curse word escaped her lips and was glad that no one was around to hear the unladylike expression. Relief was short-lived as she realized she wasn't alone. The sound of someone running down the crushed gravel path behind her let her know she wasn't.

"Please don't be my boss. Please don't be my boss," she repeated under her breath. A shadow of a man, long and broad, covered her, and she cringed, opening one eye and then the other as the person came around to her front. "Grant, thank goodness, it's you."

"It's me," he said and helped her to her feet. "I didn't know mud baths were on the schedule today." His laugh was contagious, and she giggled as she used her one clean hand to wipe the mud off her bum. Her other hand rested in his as he steadied her. "I'm only teasing you."

"What are you doing here, anyway?"

"I was on my way up for breakfast. That's my cabin right there. I've been seeing you pass my window all morning. This time, you had a whole load, and I heard the crash."

Standing in front of him, covered in mud again, she wanted to crawl under a rock for a while until the embarrassment subsided. "I'm all good here. You should go eat before it's too late." She pointed up towards the barn. "I've got some things to set up in the gazebo for yoga. Are you planning to attend this morning's activity?"

He nodded with a half-cocked grin that hid behind a day's growth of facial hair. "I can always eat later. Do you need help?"

"Thank you for offering, but I don't need help."

"You may not need it, but would you like my assistance?"

She shook her head, afraid if she opened her mouth, she'd say something that sounded ruder than she would intend. Pa had given her a slice of humble pie when she had refused his help only to find him having given it so freely anyway. Thandie didn't want a repeat of that scene anytime soon, and not with this good-looking man. "Breakfast is waiting, and you're a guest. You should get up there. I'll see you in a little while."

"Sure?"

She nodded. "Now, go."

His slightly squinted eyes and relaxed mouth made her breath catch in her chest. She bit the inside of her bottom lip as he turned up the path. He had a kind of swagger to his walk that she first noticed last night as she waited for him to walk from his cabin to the barn for dinner. He had wide-set shoulders and a trim waist like a swimmer. She caught herself as soon as she pictured him wearing tight black swim shorts, and smacked herself in the forehead. She had always had a thing for swimmers, and even if he wasn't one, she shouldn't be imagining it. He was a guest. She was a professional.

Righting her bike, she walked it back to the path. It was a longer way around, but the cart would do better on the more solid surface than it had going cross country.

Regardless of the state of the pathway, the gazebo was a mess from the overnight drizzle, and morning dew dripped from the smooth metal roof down onto the porch below. The floor space extended outwards from the main hexagonal roofed structure and was hemmed in by a spindled railing encircling five of the six sides. But the sun was peeking out, and she hoped things would dry up before the guests arrived. She checked her watch again, nearly a half hour had passed, and she had nothing to show for it.

She had brought several towels down in an earlier trip, and used one to dry the area in the center space under the roof. She didn't want the guests to be soaked from anything other than a hard workout.

It took a few more minutes to roll out thirteen matching pale-yellow yoga mats and align them to face west. She would be facing east and looking right into the sun—illuminated by the natural spotlight—but the others would have the sun at their backs. She arranged the water bottles and remaining hand towels on a section of dry railing. Taking the pastel-colored resistance bands from the bin, she placed one on each of the mats.

Everything looked great, except for her. She looked down at her favorite white leggings, now stained with green and brown from falling in the mucky grass. If that wasn't enough, her bottom and the back of her calves looked diseased from all the mud splatters she couldn't dodge during her first few trips back and forth on the bike. She was irritated that she had worn white at all, though it was one of the colors that she knew always complemented her tan skin tone and dusty brown hair. At least her matching white top with the cute crisscross straps was as crisp as ever.

Either way, she was going to need to change her leggings. Thandie took the fastest way back to her cabin, across the field that separated two rows of scrub oaks that had probably been used as property markers at some point in the past. A very fast rinse off and change of outfit was a necessity. She didn't want her boss, or the investor's scout, to see her in such a messed state. Luckily, her hair was in a pile at the top of her head and was free from dirt, but her curls had sprung into tighter twists from the morning's humidity and exertion.

No one will miss me in this bright pink outfit, she thought and smoothed a curl behind her ear in the reflection of the bathroom mirror. She added some pinky blush to the apple of her cheeks and applied some tinted lip balm, telling herself the whole time that it was just for her confidence, and not because she knew Grant would be at the gazebo soon.

CHAPTER 12

Thandie avoided getting dirty again and took the path back to the gazebo from her cabin. With two minutes to kill before the session was scheduled to begin, she sat on the center mat under the roof. Typically, during a lull in activity, she would check her phone for any notifications. It felt odd to not have the device at her fingertips. It had been nearly twenty-four hours since it fell in the mud, and until this very quiet moment, she had been too busy to even notice its absence.

Leo said he would try to fix it, and she really wanted him to fix it. If she had only hung onto her phone for a few more minutes, she could have listened to that voicemail. Davis was dead to her, but the fact that he had called and left a message would be enough to make anyone curious.

As she waited, a cloud shielded the sun, and a chill pricked at her exposed skin. She needed to get herself moving. Thandie poked her head out from the roof eaves and looked up at the parade of clouds moving eastward. "Please don't rain," she asked the sky. "You can rain later, but not now." A large drop hit her forehead and snaked down her face and neck. "Thanks for nothing."

"Do you do that a lot?" Grant's voice startled her from the other side of the gazebo. "Talk to no one?" He hopped the railing on the far side of the porch.

She shrugged and gave him a playful grin. "It's none of your business."

"I'd like to make it my business," he said and shrugged back at her.

What does that mean? she wondered. She barely knew this man, other than their rather intimate tumble on the trail. Why would he want to get to know her? Thinking of how his wide palm had cradled her head and protected it from harm was so romantic, and her heart hadn't beat so hard for a man in months. Maybe years if she was honest with herself. Davis hadn't made her flutter for a long time.

Regardless of how much Grant intrigued her, she couldn't afford to get involved with anyone. No amount of rugged appeal, nor the way he stood across from her, unbuttoning his plaid shirt and exposing his skin-tight white tee-shirt, could distract her from her work. She had a job to do. She was tasked with showing him, and all the other guests, some special attention. Neither she nor Leo knew for certain who the snoop was, though she doubted Leo meant for her to date the man for bonus points if he *was* the consultant.

The other guests hastened to her location while dodging the giant, scattered raindrops, and joined her under the roof. She counted nine. The trio of older ladies was missing in action again. Either they were not planning on participating in any activities at all, or, giving them the benefit of the doubt, they had turned back to their cabins at the first sign of rain.

"Welcome everyone. Please feel free to grab a water bottle and a towel and find a seat on any available mat. It looks like we will have a little extra room to spread out today if you'd like." She waited for them to settle in. "This morning, I'll be leading you through some restorative yoga poses. Nothing too difficult."

Thandie sat with her legs crisscrossed, facing them, and waited for everyone to mirror her. Grant found a spot to the side, in the front row. At least she wouldn't be looking him straight in his gorgeous ocean eyes for the whole duration of the activity.

"As we begin, I want you to focus on your breathing. Long, comfortable deep breaths, in and out, as we move through each position. Go ahead and take a few moments to find your rhythm. You may close your eyes if that feels better."

One by one, the guests relaxed their shoulders, closed their eyes, and breathed. She had never commanded a group so easily. These people must think highly of her and have faith in her expertise as a yoga instructor, though it was a skill that she didn't really have. After supper last night, she headed to the office and bolstered her thin knowledge of yoga, previously acquired from attending an occasional yoga class over the years, with an internet search. *How to teach yoga.* She hoped the crash course would be enough to convince these people.

She was doing nothing more than pretending, but these guests didn't need to know that. She took her cues from a yoga class that she had gone to once, where the instructor spoke in the sweetest, calm voice, and everything was stated as an invitation.

"I invite you to join me in child's pose. Focus on pressing your shoulders down and shooting your tailbone back." She got into child's pose perpendicular to the group so that they could clearly see what she was doing. The unintended consequence brought her face only a few inches from Grant's.

He smirked.

After a few breaths, she moved away from him. "Now, I invite you to push up onto your hands and knees. From here, I invite you to arch your back, pushing your belly button towards the floor and blow air through your lips. On your inhale, pull your belly button into your spine and curve your back like a cat."

She felt ridiculous. But they were totally buying into the

activity and following her instructions. She stood and walked around the space. Stopping at Margret, she asked permission to help the older woman with her posture. Anne caught Thandie's eye and nodded for her to come help too. Others in the group looked just as lost or unpracticed as Anne was.

Making her way around to the front row, she bit her lips at Grant's terrible position. She was by no means an expert, but she was also certain that if he remained in his current state, rear end pointed up, one shoulder down, and his neck cocked to one side, he would be hurting later. His pose was so bad that she suspected a ruse was underway.

He whispered up to her, "I think I need help too."

His posture was no mistake, but she played her part. She placed her hands on his hips and squared them to the floor, her touch lingering longer than it should have. Taking his neck and jaw in her fingertips, she aligned his spine and straightened his shoulders. She pointed her finger into the small of his back and pressed down lightly. "Arch. Bring your chin up. Yes. Like that," she said. "Good."

He smiled up at her with his neck extended. "That does feel better."

Thandie rolled her eyes. "I bet it does." It was clear to her that he knew, that she knew, that he was full of it.

Back at her mat, she rejoined the group on all fours. The rain gently splattered in slow drops on the roof and created a musical lullaby. The air had filled with the sweet scent from the honeysuckle hedges skirting the gazebo's railing. It was a delicious calm, even for her, and she felt it renewing something within herself.

"Now, if you can, stand on the front edge of your mat." Buzz was in the rear of the group and his daughter helped him up. Thandie waited for him to steady himself before continuing. "With your hands at your sides, face your palms forward and slowly inhale, bringing your arms in a wide circle and coming together high above your head. On the exhale, bring your hands in a large arc back down to your side."

They repeated the move for three breaths. "If you would like to modify, I invite you to lift one foot off the ground and press the toes of your free leg to your ankle on the other leg. Like a tree." Thandie bobbled finding her balance. Lucky for her, no one noticed. Except Grant, who was holding his foot against his thigh on the other leg. "Show off," she whispered. "Find your balance and repeat the breathing. Inhale, bring your arms over your head, and exhale."

She released her pose and walked around the gazebo again, helping people get their balance. Brent and Daisy were helping each other in some sort of partner move that looked less like yoga and a lot like canoodling the way the farmers' kids back home would do in the tractor on a Friday night. She couldn't help but suck in a snigger.

"Now, join me down on your mat. I invite you to lie flat and relaxed on your back." She waited for them all to change positions before she continued. "Place your open palms on the ground beside your hips and press each finger into the ground. Feel the material depress under your power. Feel your shoulders push against the floor. Breathe."

Grant cleared his throat, though it sounded like he too was stifling a laugh. She resisted the urge to look at him and see what had caused him to crack.

"Now, relax your fingers in order from your thumb to your pinky. And notice your neck and back sink further into the ground as though your bones are made of sand. And breathe."

Thandie lifted her head and saw a sea of relaxed bodies. Their chests rising and falling in slow intervals. It was hard to not feel calm in such a beautiful setting, with such sweet, aromatic air, and no digital distractions. Perhaps ruining her phone wasn't the worst thing after all.

"When you're ready, I invite you to roll to your side and push yourself into a comfortable sitting position. Bringing your feet together, let your knees fall towards the floor. Take a few healing breaths and allow your mind and your soul to be restored by this practice of self-love and connection to the earth around you."

Grant smirked as if he knew that she was making this all up as she went along. Thandie shot a glance at him and shook her head ever so slightly. There was going to be some explaining to do if he brought this up later. Which she suspected he would from the way he kept inserting himself into her day.

"When you're ready, open your eyes. Thank you for joining me this morning and I hope you enjoyed yourself. I certainly did."

"So did I," Grant said under his breath.

Ignoring him, she stood. "After lunch, there is some free time built into the schedule for a few hours. Then, at three o'clock, we will have a flower arranging class on the dock. Unless it's raining, then the class will be held in the barn."

The guests began to get up and leave.

"That was wonderful," Buzz said and walked away with his daughter by his side. Thandie was glad to see him using the walking stick, even though he hated it.

"Can we do this every morning?" A woman, maybe Clara, asked.

"You enjoyed it that much?" Thandie hid her surprise.

"I've taken a lot of yoga. Hot yoga, Yin Yoga, Vinyasa, Ashtanga, Hatha. But I've never been to a class like yours," the woman, who looked to be in her late thirties or early forties, said.

"Yeah," Grant added. "What do you call your style of yoga?"

Ignoring him again, she said, "Well, Clara, right? I can certainly look at the schedule and see where I have a spare time slot. Would you like that?"

"I would. Thank you for today. I really needed it." Clara said and looked over her shoulder at a man who was rolling the yellow mats.

It was obvious to anyone who had been in love before that Clara and the man had some sort of connection, but one that was strained under an invisible force. If Thandie's yoga class was helping them in any tangible way, her pretending was very much worth the show that she had put on.

"Do you want help cleaning up?" Anne asked and began collecting water bottles.

Thandie rushed to Anne and stood between her and the trash. "Thank you for the offer, but I can handle all this. And I'll see you all a little later."

The rain, having stopped sometime while she was melting into her mat, left the ground damp around the gazebo. The sun peeked back through a break in the clouds and vaporized the sitting water. The humidity rose like steam and the sweet air was replaced by a thick haze that made her feel like taking a nap. But there were things to do, and a nap would have to wait. She straightened her spine and smiled at Margret, who was coming right at her.

"This was brilliant," Margret said and shook Thandie's hand. "You are a gem."

Thandie didn't know what to say, although she felt an urge to admit the truth to the kind woman. But she didn't. "It was my pleasure. I'm glad you liked it."

Grant joined them.

"And did you enjoy yourself this morning?" Margret asked him and nudged him closer towards Thandie.

"Very much," he said.

"What was your favorite part?" Margret said as she pulled Anne away in a not very subtle goodbye.

Thandie waved her fingers at the two friends, knowing exactly what they were up to. Grant cleared his throat, and she met his gaze. His beautiful oceanic orbs pierced into her like Triton's staff. "Dare I ask what your favorite part was?" she said and felt a butterfly flutter in her belly.

"My favorite part?" Grant leaned into her. His fingers rested gently on her shoulder as he whispered. "When you faked being a yoga instructor."

Thandie pushed him away. "Oh, you! You are the absolute . . . " *Worst*, she would have finished, but remembered her place. Her job was to make him fall in love with the retreat, not her. She put some more space between them and busied herself with the cleanup.

"What am I?" he said and approached her where she was rolling the mats and stacking them. "I said, what am I? Finish your thought."

"You're teasing me."

"I am," Grant said and helped her load the mats into the cart hitched to her bike.

"I don't need your help. But thank you," she said and wrestled the mats away from his grip.

"What am I?" he repeated with a grin that she either wanted to slap off or kiss.

She stopped loading and dropped the items from her hands. She swallowed hard and thought of any answer other than the truth. He was handsome. He was funny. He was driving her as crazy as a squirrel riding on an eagle's back.

His hand caught hers by her side and he nudged her chin up to see his face better. She wet her lips. Her body was responding to him. It was primal. It was too fast. And it wasn't real.

Thandie backed away. "You are complicating things for me," she said, and it was the truth.

He took a step backwards. His wounded pride radiated off his stiff body. Grant nodded as though he understood her, and the pained look on his face tore at her. He combed his fingers back through his wavy hair and looked out into the sun. Into a distant past that she knew nothing about.

"I'll see you later?" she asked, but he turned up the path without answering her, cold in the squareness of his shoulders.

She was left in the gazebo wondering what the heck had just happened. One second, they were playfully teasing, and the next, it was as though he'd seen a ghost.

CHAPTER 13

"This is bad. Very, very bad." Thandie said and smoothed her frizzy curls away from her face.

She paced along the gazebo's railing, occasionally picking up a mat or a towel and throwing the items into the cart. What was she supposed to do, let him embrace her? And then what? Where would that lead? Thandie stomped on the wooden planks and stood erect. "I am an employee here. He is a guest. No matter how much I like the man, I must keep a professional distance. If not for my sake, then for Leo's."

With renewed resolve, she tossed the few remaining things into the cart and headed to the barn, where she hoped Grant would not be. She was embarrassed. Again. Grant's advance had been inappropriate, given their roles, but she had to admit, it wasn't unprovoked. Heck, he probably thought all the attention she was giving to him was a kind of flirting!

"This is bad," she repeated as she mounted her bicycle and began up the path.

Ahead, the darkened barn was like an abyss, waiting to devour her. She pedaled backwards, slowing to a stop. With her feet planted on the ground on either side of the bike, she took a couple of much-needed deep breaths. "If I make it through this week, I'll need a wellness retreat myself," she said and resumed her journey back to the barn.

The pressure to do what she had to do to help The Foundry and keep her job was more than she had expected it to be. She wished she had never heard Leo and America discussing the investor situation at all. She could have done her job just fine not knowing that so much was riding on her performance.

While replaying her interaction with Grant over and over in her mind, and dissecting where she had gone wrong, she easily made the half-dozen trips up to the loft. She put away all the mats and the bands she had neglected to utilize during her improvised yoga session. If she got a chance to redo the activity, she would find some way to incorporate more equipment and switch things up.

Back outside, Pa crouched beside her bicycle. He fumbled through a tool bag and what sounded like a pile of metal wrenches and screw drivers banging against one another. Like a magician, he held the thing he needed up in front of his grinning face before hunching over and doing something to the cart.

"Hey, Pa," she said from the door so as not to startle him.

He looked up over the top rim of his safety glasses. "Did she work?"

"The cart? I hate to admit, but your fix was better than what I had rigged up."

"Well, she just needs a little tuning up, and if that golfcart is a far way out, I can do a bit of fabricating and get this thing properly connected." Pa clapped his hands together and rubbed one greasy palm on his worn khaki coveralls, which looked to be an army surplus uniform. "I know you aren't the kind of woman who needs help, but let me know if anything comes up."

"I understand," she said and helped him with his heavy tool bag, though he carried it like it was nothing more than a sack of air. "Pa, can I ask you something?"

"Shoot," he said and made his fingers into the shape of a cap-gun. He laughed like a jolly Santa mixed with the gruffness of a life hard-lived.

"What is it about this place?" Thandie said. "There's so much energy and optimism in the air, even among the guests."

Pa smiled upside down. Her question stumped him, perhaps. He paused and threaded both arms through the tool bag's handle. "It wasn't like this before."

"Before what?"

"I take it back," Pa said. "It was like this a long time ago. But after the cove dried up, people moved away. Everyone that *did* stay accepted that the good days were behind them and did nothing to create change. But then, America showed up here and flipped the whole place on its head. There was a big fancy resort looking to build in the area, but after we came together, they couldn't get what they wanted. We found our joy again and rediscovered what it means to be a community. A real one where people lift each other up instead of tearing things down."

"Reminds me of home."

"Where's that?" Pa asked.

"A little town near Omaha, but on the Iowa side."

"Ah, corn country. Do you miss it?"

"I miss some of my friends. My parents. But I'm not ready to go back anytime soon," Thandie admitted, though she was unaccustomed to saying it out loud.

"Sounds like a story there."

She nodded.

"Uh oh." Pa pointed with his chin. "That story will have to wait for another time. Here comes the boss."

Leo came through the doors carrying a large stack of white, freshly laundered towels. "Just the person I was looking for. How was the morning's activity?"

"Good. It drizzled, but the gazebo kept us all dry, and the

sound and scent of the rain were relaxing," Thandie said. "What do you need?"

Leo handed her the towels, still warm from the dryer. "I need you to take these to the Bear Cabin."

"Isn't that Grant—I mean, Mr. Goldie's cabin?"

"You got it," he said.

"I'm happy to deliver these, but—"

"But what? Is everything going as you planned?" Leo asked and his face tensed with concern.

Thandie didn't want to give him anything more to worry about than he already had on his plate. "Everything is great. I'll take these right away." She placed them in the cart.

"Where did you get this contraption?" Leo pointed to the cart on her bike.

She nodded at Pa, who was beaming.

"I did it," Pa said. "Your director here was having a time of it getting her things down to the gazebo. And I needed something fun to do other than dig that drainage trench behind the barn. Do you like what I came up with?"

"Nice work, Pa. I owe you one."

"I'll add it to your tab," he said as he walked away. "But, for you, Thandie, this one's on the house."

"Thanks, Pa," Thandie said and smirked as though she'd won a prize.

"What's on the schedule for this afternoon?" Leo asked from the door.

"Flower arranging." Thandie threw her leg over the rear tire and sat down on the bike seat. "And then supper."

"Sounds good," Leo said. "Now get going."

Looking at the fast-moving gray clouds hovering low in the sky, Thandie knew she needed to hurry if she were going to get the towels to Grant's cabin while they were still fresh—and dry. She pedaled and let gravity pull her and the cart down the path. Grant's cabin was situated closer to the old shoreline than the one where she was staying, and between the barn and the gazebo.

Thankfully when she came around the back side of his cabin, it looked empty. She could just put the towels right inside and skedaddle before accidentally having another encounter with *him*. Not now. She needed to focus on all the guests, not only Grant, but he was making it hard for her to do anything other than that. *He's just so good-looking*, she thought, swooning.

Taking the stack of towels in hand, she knocked.

While she waited, she looked over her shoulder to the dancing wildflowers. The lady trio walked by on the path and waved. Thandie pressed the pile of towels to her chest with one hand and waved back to them. "Heading up for lunch?"

One of them nodded and pointed up the ramble. With the sun shining through puffy white and gray clouds in quick passing intervals and a steady breeze, it was a beautiful time of day for the quarter-mile walk, though she would have taken a bike or an umbrella at a minimum if she were them.

Thandie knocked again. With no answer, she used her master key and entered the front door. "Hello?" she called out, just in case Grant was in there. The Bear Cabin was so unlike hers. The walls were made of rolled logs with white chinking. The window frames were painted white to match. A round iron chandelier hung from a long wooden beam at the peak of the ceiling. Despite its small size, the studio space had a cozy appeal.

Beside the entry was a coatrack and a sitting area with two oversized leather chairs and a small game table. A kitchen was tucked into one corner, and a bed and desk made up the opposite side of the room. It was so quaint, but now she felt as though she was violating his privacy by being essentially inside of his bedroom.

A door hung ajar near the kitchen, and she could see a white glossy bathtub and a porcelain pedestal sink with brass legs. She walked in and looked for a place to put the extra towels. Behind the door, she found a narrow linen cabinet and opened it. Inside, she discovered all of his toiletries on the top shelf, in addition to a stack of perfectly good, folded white towels.

She closed the doors and placed the extra towels where he could see them on the back of the toilet tank. There was no way he hadn't seen the extra towels on the shelf below his personal things! Curious, she opened the door again and inventoried the other shelves. One held several rolls of toilet tissue and a small tray of complimentary toiletry items, such as shampoo and lotion.

The bottommost shelf was left empty. She straightened the rolls and existing towels in their designated places, but paused at the top shelf. A tortoiseshell comb lay perfectly perpendicular to the front edge, and his toothbrush lay in the center of a long, narrow dish. His deodorant, face cream, lotion, hair gel, and under-eye moisturizer stood like little toy soldiers in a row.

He was meticulous, she had to give him that.

"Ahem," a voice broke her snooping, and she whipped around. "Hi." Grant gave a wave with his fingers.

The cabinet doors clattered, and items toppled over inside as the door latched. "Um. Hello," she said. "I was just—um— bringing you extra towels."

"I hoped you would," he said.

"You did? Why?"

"I felt really bad about how I behaved earlier. You have a job to do here, and I took advantage of that," Grant admitted, though it wasn't quite an apology for the way he recoiled and stormed away from the gazebo.

Something twisted in her stomach. "I hadn't noticed anything," she said. "Just two adults enjoying each other's company. However, I do have a job to do. I put your towels just in there and please let me, or any of the other staff, know how we can make your stay here more enjoyable."

She was proud of how professional, though slightly cold, she sounded.

"So," he met her in the middle of the room, his bedroom, and took her by the hands. Warm hands. "There's nothing between us?"

His question had several meanings. She felt the electricity turn every hair on her arms on end. There was something between them, but admitting that out loud would ruin everything. She couldn't chance losing her job. She pulled her hands away and broke their connection. His eyes lowered ever so slightly at the sudden parting.

"Grant, I can't. And if things were different, I think I'd like to get to know you better, like why you line up all your toiletries, that no one else is going to see, in perfect little rows, or why you know more about yoga than I do, or what a man like you is doing at a wellness retreat, alone, in the first place. But that would be out of place for me."

"I line up my toiletries because I like order." He paused and closed the distance between them. "I spent a year in Bali learning yoga from a master guru." He brushed a ringlet behind her ear. "And I think I'd like to know you better, too."

"In a professional way," she said quickly and hid the quiver in her voice.

"Of course," he said and moved out of the way of the door. "Will I see you later?"

"Flower arranging at the dock at three. Then supper. Tomorrow, we'll have breakfast outdoors. I've got something really fun planned."

"And the bonfire tomorrow night?" Grant asked as she brushed by him.

His hand fell to her elbow, and she paused looking into his eyes. Her breath caught at his touch. "It looks like rain," she said and put her hand out the door. A drop, and then another landed in her hand. "Wear your poncho."

CHAPTER 14

Grant had skipped the flower arranging event and dinner. He knew better than to miss an opportunity to scout out The Foundry, but he held back. Instead of doing his job, he chose to cower alone in his room all afternoon. This woman, Thandie, had captured his imagination like no other person had done since he had lost so much.

He was utterly distracted from why he was even there. Their shared moments together had been a refreshing realization. For the first time in nearly a decade, he could see a reason for possibly dismantling the walls around his heart. There was no reason he couldn't do both his job and explore the crack rapidly forming in his defenses.

Grant stood from the picnic table where breakfast had just wrapped up and helped Margret and Anne slide out from the bench. He noticed the awkward bench braces that hindered one's ability from scooting out with any kind of grace and felt it was probably time for the resort to make an upgrade. His new friends' jovial spirits had made his trip so much more fun than he had on a typical consulting job, and breakfast had been no exception. Though Thandie hadn't made an appearance, he had been thoroughly entertained and stuffed.

Light, wispy clouds had shaded them during their breakfast of fresh fruit cut into various flower forms and an array of baked goods made to resemble little ducks, eggs, twigs, and more. Now the sun burned through the high-level haze and cut a line of light down the pathway towards the dock.

"What happened after you fell into the creek?" Grant asked Margret, wanting to know the rest of the story. "Did you find the coin?"

"My feet planted in the sticky mud at the bottom of the stream. It was shallow, maybe a half meter, but I couldn't move. It was as though the mud had wrapped a million ropes about my ankle. I was stuck."

Three other women joined in on listening to her tale as they made their way to the dock. "How did you get out?" one of them asked.

"I've heard this story a hundred times," Anne said. "I'll meet you down there." She speed walked with her hips swinging from side to side and separated herself from the group.

"So?" one of the other women asked and nudged her way between Grant and Margret.

"I yelled for help, knowing that my companion was nearby searching the banks further downstream. After a panicked quarter hour, I realized no one was coming anytime soon. I began to wiggle my foot ever so slowly as not to create suction underneath. I felt the pressure around my ankle begin to give way as the stream moved the fine silt under my rising boot. When I got it about halfway out, I moved my cupped hand through the water just above my ankle and swooshed the muck from around my trapped toes. When I brought my hand up, peeking out from the slippery black sludge . . . gold."

"Gold what?" a woman asked.

"It was a coin. And it shone in the late-day sun like the day it was struck," Margret beamed at the retelling. "I cupped it in my hands and dunked it in the passing water until it came out completely clean. Oh my! It was a beauty."

"What kind of coin was it?" Grant asked, now that he was totally in the grips of her story. "Do you still have it?"

"It was exactly what I had been out there looking for in that bog. The coin dated back nearly five hundred years. I must have shouted with such exuberance at the find, that my partner heard me and arrived on site. He helped me out of the creek and we both just sat there staring at the golden piece."

Margret opened her small bag and dug around inside. Grant wondered why this woman would be carrying around an ancient gold coin in her purse, but waited with excitement to see the object. At this point in Margret's story, she pulled out a small leather envelope and the whole group crowded around to see the coin.

With practiced drama, she untied the twine and opened one flap. "Do you want to see it?" She toyed with them, drawing out the moment further than necessary, but for effect, and Grant appreciated the theatrical flair.

"Show us," Grant said. "You've kept us waiting for long enough."

With her fingers dipping into the opening, she presented, not a gold coin, but a photograph. Barely in color, it was so faded. But he could make out her younger self with long blonde hair, standing on the bank of a river, and holding a gold coin to the camera.

"You don't have it?" Grant said with disappointment evident in his cracking voice.

"Of course not. I sold it, and the others. How else do you think I can afford to travel all year round?" Margret said and replaced the photograph back in its home after they each looked.

"The others? You found more coins?"

"Several," she said. "We found more on the side of the riverbank where I had been stuck. The find was one of the greatest moments of my life."

"I bet," another woman, whom he hadn't been introduced to yet, said as they reached the dock.

"Now you know why I didn't need to hear this again," Anne said. She sat on the bench that was built-in along the side of the old dock's railing.

"Why didn't you warn us?" Grant joked to Anne.

Anne laughed. "She pays my bills. I have to allow her a bit of fun."

More footsteps trailed the group down the dock's weathered planks, and Grant's pulse quickened as he hoped to see Thandie. He turned, smile already in place. It wasn't Thandie. It was the old man whose name he could not remember. He ran the ones that sounded right through his head. Ted? Ken? Ben? Buzz? He snapped his fingers. Buzz was the correct name he was searching for.

Buzz waved and skip-walked with his cane to Margret's side as though they were old friends. Their conversation picked up where one had previously left off, and Grant was completely lost. He bowed out of their repartee and walked to the end of the dock where an unpainted section of railing looked to have recently been added.

Leaning over the edge, he could see where a ladder had once been attached for climbing in and out of the lake. The exposed lakebed was only a yard below his feet, but he could still imagine kids cannonballing into the warm summer waters. Even now, the sun heated the flesh on the back of his neck and arms the way he knew he needed after a long winter without getting much sun.

Sun was preferable to the damp conditions of the previous morning. Despite the less-than-ideal weather, the staff had planned for and thought of everything. The gravel path was well drained and easy to walk on, even in the rain. There were more umbrellas and ponchos than any guest might need. Many of the cabins boasted wide covered porches, and the activities had, so far, worked well in the environment. This report to Davis would be balanced and show that the apparent drawbacks of the property might actually be advantages.

The last of the guests moseyed down the dock and joined the rest, who were already there and waiting for their activity to begin. He checked his watch out of habit and looked around for any sign of Thandie.

"Come join me down here," Thandie's voice cut through the air from down the shore a way. "What are you all waiting for?"

He could hear her smile even though she was far away, and the sun was too bright against her back for him to see her clearly. Whatever she had in store for them, he hoped it would be as good as yesterday's events. His favorite event, of course, had been the little rendezvous in his cabin. Asking her to bring towels that he didn't need may have crossed the line, but he wanted to see her so that he could offer an apology. He could have just been honest, but he didn't think she would come willingly if there wasn't a good reason.

In the gazebo, he had let his body do the thinking. When Thandie pulled away, his past crashed into his soul and guilt flooded his veins. She would never understand. How could she?

With refreshed boundaries, and having skipped the flower arranging, it was crucial that he not miss any more activities. They had agreed to get to know each other more *on a professional level*, and he still had a job to do.

Grant took up the rear of the pack behind the old man with the cane, Buzz, and allowed the others to get to Thandie first. After all, they were all real guests, wanting a relaxing experience. Whereas he hadn't even paid for the privilege of being there. Taking up the rear gave him a better vantage point to take-in and take note of the whole scene.

"Thank you all for coming here. Today, we are going to

practice a type of meditation. As you can see, I have brought some supplies for your use today. What you'll do is take a mat and find a quiet spot along this stretch. Find a comfortable seat," she pointed to a chair and nodded to Buzz, "and using the materials within your reach, you'll create a stacked stone sculpture called a cairn."

Thandie picked up two mats by their bungee strap. When her eyes came back to the group, they swept over the tops of the heads in front of Grant and landed squarely on his face. "I see you back there," she said.

A slight hesitation in her voice, barely perceivable, and a shake of her head, like a chill had just run down her spine, caused him to bite his lower lip. He certainly had an effect on her. There was no use in denying it anymore, but it was yet to be seen whether the effect was a good or bad thing.

"Why don't you come down to the front and demonstrate for me." Thandie waved him forward.

What was he supposed to do? A different kind of heat warmed his neck, but not from the sun—from his rising anxiety. There was a reason he preferred to take up the rear, sit in the back of the classroom, and by no means did he want to demonstrate anything to anyone. She gave him a smirk, and the side-tilt of her chin encouraged him to come up. He obliged her request.

The group broke out into applause as he moved between them and took a mat from Thandie's hand. Taking a bow, Grant couldn't help but chuckle at the anxiety he had just felt. It was ridiculous. He was ridiculous. These people looking at him had nothing but good vibes towards him, but even still, he wanted to hide under a rock, not stack them.

Being nervous wouldn't serve him now. He took a deep breath as he came beside Thandie. Seeing the tension in his face, she placed her soft fingers on his forearm and calmed him further. "Okay. Okay. What do you want me to do?" Grant asked and unrolled the mat.

"Now, take a seat."

Grant flopped the rubber mat onto the ground and sat, but as soon as his bottom hit the surface, he was right back up again. "Ouch." He laughed without humor and rubbed his bottom where something goosed him. Folding the mat back, he revealed a rather pointed stone sticking up from the place where he had attempted to sit. He kicked the errant stone away and tried sitting again, this time with more success.

"Now, reach for three stones of various sizes. Taking the largest one, place it in front of you so that it has no wobble," she said, and he acted out her instructions. "Now, take the medium-sized stone and balance it on top of the first."

Grant caught on right away. Though he'd never taken part in any Zen rock stacking before, the concept was one that every kindergartner would be familiar with. "I got it," he said as he balanced the remaining stone.

Thandie clapped, having joined the others for a better vantage point. "Very good," she said. "Now, this was the most basic example and certainly a good place to start. But I want you to challenge yourself with this meditation. Remember, this experience is only for you. With each rock you place, you will assign something to it that you need to let go of. I want you to see that, as the structure rises, your negative thoughts, your trauma, and your vices together can be turned into something beautiful."

Behind Thandie, Margret raised her hand. Grant pointed in that direction, causing Thandie to turn around and face the group.

"Questions?" she said.

"Hypothetically, what if we don't have anything that we need to let go of?" Margret asked.

Anne nudged her friend and put up a palm to Thandie like a crossing guard. "Thandie, I got this." She looked Margret straight on and took her shoulders in her hands. "Listen to me very carefully. Nobody, not even you, is perfect enough to have nothing they need to let go of. Even Gandhi, as good a man as he was, let go of his shoes. You will sit there, and you will build a tower of all the things wrong with you."

Margret was slack-jawed at the rebuke, and Grant held in his amusement with his lips between his teeth.

CHAPTER 15

Having handled her friend so fully, Anne nodded to Thandie and spoke under her breath. "May I suggest you begin with your ego?" The two women traded friendly shoulder nudges and caused the other to laugh.

Thandie held in her giggle. "Any more questions?" She waited a moment.

A hand went up from the rear of the group. "Do we get to eat when we're through?" one of the trio asked.

"Snacks are on the way down and will be served by the dock. Now, grab your mat and fan out. If you need assistance, I'll be walking amongst you all. All you need to do is ask me." Thandie clapped her hands and felt a smile spread across her face. She wasn't sure about adding this activity to the schedule at first, but as the guests' eyes lit up while taking their mats, she could see that it already had promise. "And don't forget to have fun with it."

"I could use some help," Grant said, leaning back on his elbows with his ankles crossed out in front of him like he was sunbathing. He tugged lightly on her leg, and she sat beside him on one side of his mat.

"That's what I'm here for. What do you need help with, Grant

Goldie?" She spoke quietly until the guests had made their way further along the old shore.

"I need . . . I want to know you."

A blush heated her cheeks at his bold declaration. "I don't think that's very professional."

"No, it's not," he said.

She was afraid to look at him and be sucked into the smoldering gaze that she could feel on her skin. She remembered her job again and what was at stake. "I'm not promising that I'll answer, but you may ask me one thing."

"Your name. Is there a story there?" Grant turned her chin towards his face.

"Yes."

"That's all I get?" he whined.

She shrugged and played coy, but couldn't resist his pathetic pouting for long. "I was named after my grandmother, Thandeka. She was the only person in the family who supported my parents being a mixed-race couple. She passed away and my parents fled from South Africa shortly before I was born."

"That sounds like a whole other story."

"And maybe you'll get to hear it someday." She batted her lashes in a slightly too smug sort of way. "The kids in school called me Thandie for short, and it just stuck. I like it. It's a good conversation starter."

Grant grunted his agreement. "I appreciate you telling me. And now that I've gotten my one answer, you should probably check on the others. I've stolen enough of your time."

Thandie stood and brushed off the small bits of gravel that had stuck into her palms. "Get to stacking."

"Yes, ma'am," he said and grinned, his eyes wrinkled above his cheeks. "Thanks for sitting with me for a moment."

"Anytime," she said and turned around quickly to walk away. *Anytime?* What was she thinking? Although crossing a professional line with Grant was not going to happen, she was having a difficult time remembering that she was an employee at the retreat, and he was a guest. Their little conversations and stolen moments felt like little dates. The best dates she had ever been on.

Perhaps the clear line, the one she was not going to cross, took some of the pressure off of talking with him. And she did enjoy talking with him. She enjoyed looking at him, too. His rugged stubble, strong jaw, and bright eyes were more attractive the more she saw him. She liked the skintight tees he wore under unbuttoned plaid shirts every day. And his cargo khakis hugged his bum in all the right places. She wondered if admiring his form was a sin, because it felt so naughty.

Thandie shook the raw image from her head. She really needed to stop thinking of Grant in such a familiar way. She bent down and placed a square stone on a flat one in honor of the thing she needed to let go of. There was no reason to have hope that she and Grant could be anything more than what they were in the vacuum of their situation.

"What are you stacking for?" the man with the baritone voice asked from down the way, though he was the closest guest to where she had stopped.

"William, right?"

He nodded and asked his question again.

Thandie wagged her finger over her tiny tower. "You know I can't tell you that. Do you need help with yours?"

William leaned to one side on his mat and revealed his rather large tower.

"That's impressive," she said as she counted the stones in his stack. There were easily a dozen stones to his cairn. Her curiosity was piqued, and she really wanted to know what all of his layers represented, though she dared not ask. "Did you know you were such a natural at this?"

He chuckled. "I don't know if I should be happy at this, or depressed at all the things that I need to let go of."

"Well, this is an exercise on introspection, and I suspect you've already begun to let go of some of those things, whether you realize it yet or not."

"You want to know?" William tapped his fingers along the edge of each stone causing the tower to waggle, though it didn't tip over.

Thandie waved her hands. "Oh, no. This is for you." But her grin gave her away, and he called her over.

"You know the woman who I'm here with? Clara? We were engaged once. A long time ago. Every one of these stones represents a time that I decided not to call her. A time that I drove by her house and didn't stop. A time when I should have apologized and didn't. A time when I could have been a better man for her."

"You're here trying to rekindle your—"

"Trying to heal. Yes," he said. "And I think this is a good start."

"I do too," Clara's voice stole William and Thandie's attention from behind them. She pointed at her stack of equal height. "I had the same idea."

Thandie, realizing this was now a very private moment between two people in need of each other, backed away. The couple embraced as though they had each thought of the moment for a hundred years. It was sweet, and real, and beautiful. Thandie quietly wished them well and moved further down the way towards the other guests.

Margret was quick to wave Thandie over and present her stack for approval. With a wide grin and Vanna White hands, she said, "Well, what do you think?" The stack was made up of two towers, each four stones tall. A skinny, flat rock bridged the towers with three more placed on top at the center. One final round stone balanced at the apex like a head about to roll off a tiny body.

"What is it?" Thandie asked, genuinely curious.

"It's Anne. Don't you see the likeness?"

"I heard that," Anne shouted from somewhere nearby.

"Good." Margret shot back. "I said I didn't have anything I needed to let go of, except maybe her."

"I heard that too. Now come look at mine," Anne said.

Thandie helped Margret to her feet, and they made their way toward where Anne's voice had come from behind a clump of shrubs. When they came around the foliage, Thandie was unable to hold in her giggle. Anne had stacked a similar, albeit much larger structure, that had an uncanny resemblance to Margret.

"I'll be damned, if that doesn't look just like . . ." Margret covered her mouth as she realized that Anne's stacked stones were positioned in her likeness.

"I think you two missed the point of this meditation," Thandie said and stood between them. "Are you two always like this, with the jabs and teasing?"

"When you've known someone as long as we have, it just makes life more fun when you don't take things so seriously," Anne said.

"I whole-heartedly concur," Margret added.

Thandie looked around at the other guests, who were beginning to stand and check out the other guests' cairns. "Looks like everyone is about through. Why don't you make your way back soon? I'll check on the snacks."

In the shadow of the dock, the chef had delivered a delicious charcuterie spread, complete with a pitcher of sparkling sangria and a plate of chocolates. She wanted to dive right in but knew the guests' needs came first. With any luck, there would be some leftovers to munch on while she cleaned up from the activity.

If not, she fully planned on hunting down the chef, introducing herself properly, and requesting a mini version to enjoy later in her cabin. The chef was an enigma, popping in and out without being spotted, all the while preparing the most mouth-watering food she had eaten in her life.

"What's for lunch?" William said, with a very smiley Clara on his arm.

"Oh," Thandie said and moved away from the table. "This is just a snack. Lunch will be served at two in the *cucina*. Help yourself. Did you enjoy your meditations?"

The two forty-somethings touched noses. "I think this was exactly the breakthrough we both needed," Clara said. "Sometimes you just hold on to things for so long that you forget that you can let them go."

"Amen to that!" Thandie said. The woman's sentiment rang true in more than one way.

Thandie wondered if she was holding on too tightly to the hurt, the anger, and the humiliation that had been weighing her down for months. Running away from it all had only added to her burden. Now she was broke *and* broken.

Taking a cue from Clara, and heeding her own advice, Thandie knew that she was in control of either holding on or letting go. Davis made his choice when he left her, and she had chosen to beat herself up over it ever since. Thandie was done holding onto his mistakes any longer.

She raced back to where she had stacked the one stone. Passing Grant on her way, he attempted to stop her by holding her arm, but she breezed by him.

"Where's the fire?" Grant yelled as she ran past.

There was no time to answer him. There was no time to explain, or even a desire to do so. She knew what she needed to do. She slowed as she reached the spot where her tiny little rock sat on another, and she kicked them apart. That act alone was renewing. She had assigned the wrong thing to the poor rock.

This time, as she carefully selected the best rocks, flat and not too smooth, she spoke the hurts aloud. "Broken relationships. Lost time. Feeling sorry for myself. All the tears, wasted." She gathered a few more stones and added them to this list. "Kisses, wasted. Laughs we never truly shared because you were too serious to understand me. Goodbye Davis," she said as she stacked the seventh stone. It balanced, but not well. She took one more that had a slight concave side. "Davis," she said again for good measure as she placed the apex stone on the cairn.

"Who's Davis?" Grant asked, having caught up to her.

"No one now." Thandie stood and looked at her tower, feeling much lighter than she had a few minutes ago, and much lighter than she had been feeling for months. She swiped the dirt from her hands and placed them on her hips. "You know how this could be better?"

Grant's face said he had an idea but didn't want to say it out loud. He shrugged his shoulders and nudged her to continue with a single chin nod.

She knew what she needed to do, though she hesitated. Her stack of rocks, each one representing the things she wanted so badly to let go of, the things she *needed* to let go of if she were ever to move on, stared back at her, begging for her to reconsider. "No more," she said and kicked the stones as hard as she could. Her days playing soccer in grade-school came in clutch as the stones flew through the air and scattered amongst the pebbled old shore and long grasses. Her trauma and regrets came to rest in obscurity where the stones met the wildflowers dancing in the sunlight.

Applause echoed off the stones. She turned around and her cheeks heated at the sight of several guests watching the unplanned entertainment. She could do nothing but make the most of it. "That felt better than I thought it would." She laughed.

"All I know is I would not want to be *Davis* right now," Grant quipped.

Thandie let out a deep breath. She *was* ready to move on. "Thank you all for coming today, and I'll see you back down here at sundown for the bonfire."

"Can I help you clean up?" Grant asked. "I know I shouldn't, but I want to."

"No. I can handle it—"

"I'm not taking no for an answer."

Something about the way he took charge didn't intimidate her. His was a genuine offer and suggested in no way that he thought her incapable of doing her job. He really just wanted to help, and maybe it was time she let him.

CHAPTER 16

Had Grant heard Thandie correctly? There had to be a million people named Davis in the world. But no matter the improbability that *her* Davis and *his* boss were one and the same, he had to admit the possibility was there. While he had helped her put away the mats and the food, he wanted to ask her. He had steered the conversation toward work, toward her past, even asking if she was single, but hadn't been brave enough to ask the question that he wanted answered most. What had Davis, whoever he was, done to her?

He doubted she would ever tell him, now that she had let go of the hurt that she had been carrying with a spectacular kick that sent her cairn flying into the grass. Her whole dramatic display only proved to him that he knew nothing about women in general, but he had an overwhelming sense that he was supposed to know this one.

Everything his soul was telling him to do flew in the face of what he knew he should be doing. He was to get in, do the assessment, and get out. No one should know who he is, and he should not remember any of the people he conversed with. Small talk was the game, and he was failing on an epic scale.

The more he got to know Margret, Anne, and the other guests, the more connected he felt to everything around him. The Foundry wasn't just a collection of cabins beside an empty lake with seemingly random activities and an activities director that was either genius or totally making up things as she went along. It was showing itself as a place of hope and renewal.

One thing he was certain about was that if this place could make even Grant Goldie come out of his broken shell, it was something special, to be sure.

Grant checked his outfit in the oval bathroom mirror hanging above the sink. His gray-and-blue flannel shirt was perfect for the bonfire. He would be warm enough, but not too hot. He buttoned the shirt all the way up, stopping at the top button and deciding to leave it open for a more casual look. He tucked in the hem and re-zipped his fly.

"Nope," he said to himself, and untucked the shirt from his pants. No matter how many times he tried, he just didn't like the way he looked stiff and unnatural when his shirt was tucked in. *Plus*, he reminded himself, *it's only a bonfire*. It would be dark and cool.

He sprayed cologne on his chest and shook his shirt to disperse the scent. Pleased with his appearance, he reset his toiletries on the little cabinet shelf and folded his towel in perfect thirds before hanging it on the bar beside the shower.

His stomach growled, having skipped dinner. He had taken a nap instead of attending the meal. A snooze was always a good idea, though he couldn't remember the last time he had actually taken one. His alarm went off an hour before the bonfire and he killed time with showering, cleaning up his stubble, and second-guessing his shirt choice.

What he was really second-guessing was whether he was being a fool about Thandie. She was beyond kind, not only to him, but to all the guests. She was patient and thoughtful. The way she invited everyone to participate in the events, without ever appearing pushy or intimidating, spoke to the sort of woman she was inside or outside of work.

Right now, she was at work, likely setting up for the bonfire and making sure everything was taken care of for the guests. Though he shouldn't feel bad, as he was a guest at the retreat, he wondered if he should have helped her with the bonfire. Relaxing wasn't something he did well, and as far as anyone else was concerned, he was a man needing wellness at a quiet upstate retreat.

That part was half true. The nap had been much needed, and he was glad that he had taken a few hours for himself. The moments to do so were few and far between with his job. He was always on the way to some new place at some ungodly hour and typically felt pride in his go-go-go attitude toward life. This particular assignment was affording him an opportunity to rest while still doing his work. He could lean into it, or he could over-work himself into a heartless report for Mr. Mothan and miss out on really experiencing the rest of the week.

It wasn't easy to miss that Thandie was working harder than anyone else he knew, and he wondered when or if she got time to rest. He was glad that he had not taken no for an answer, and lightened her load, even for a little while, and that made him feel warm inside. He hadn't helped her because he wanted something in return, and he hadn't helped her so that he could hear some inside scoop about the inner workings of The Foundry and add to his report. He hadn't lent a hand to win her over.

He had simply listened to his heart and helped someone who would never have asked.

As a schoolboy grin pulled at his cheeks, he poured himself a small glass of cold water. Downing it in one gulp, he wiped the drops from the corner of his mouth and placed the glass in the sink. With one last check in the mirror, he opened the cabin's door and nearly stumbled over a tray sitting at the threshold. A note on top read, "Thought you might be hungry. Enjoy," and he knew it was from Thandie.

The tray held a white dinner plate covered in aluminum foil, and a single little bottle of red wine. He took the tray, looked down the path in hopes of glimpsing her, and brought it inside to the kitchen counter. He could smell the earthy scent of a buttery filet mignon and roasted potatoes before he even peeked under the hood. He placed the plate in the fridge with every intention of digging in following the bonfire.

Which he was now late getting to.

Grant left his cabin and followed the gravel path toward the old dock. Like a beacon, the fire illuminated the space with an orange glow and silhouetted some of the guests as they moved around the flames.

He spotted Thandie long before he reached her. She was radiant. Her skin glowed like a sunset, and her jeans and white t-shirt were the most attractive things he'd seen her wear. She knew how to pull off the wholesome, all-American, drop-dead-gorgeous-without-even-trying thing so well. He swallowed hard, realizing that she was way out of his league.

Margret came up behind him and linked her arm through his. His hand reached across and naturally fell to the older woman's. "What's a good-looking guy like you doing here all alone? I don't want to hear any tale about you needing to find yourself."

"I told you—"

"The truth?" she pressed.

Grant leaned in and whispered, "I'm a spy. But you can't tell anyone."

Margret released her hold on his arm. "And why would you tell me something like that? I don't believe it for a moment," Margret said. "Anne, Anne. He said he's a spy." She laughed as she walked toward her friend.

Technically he hadn't fibbed. He was spying on the establishment in order to ascertain its profit potential. But

Margret didn't need to know that. Nor Anne, or anyone else, especially Leo or Thandie. He laughed at having exposed his true reason for being there and for the delightful fact that no one would believe it.

"What's so funny?" Thandie said.

When had she noticed him standing there? Thandie jumped in front of him with a wide smile and bright eyes gracing her face. "Hi," he said.

"Hi."

He brushed the back of his hand down the length of her arm and lingered where their fingers touched by her side. A little shiver ran through her at his touch, but he could tell by her pinched brow that she was unsure how to feel about the way her body reacted to him. For that matter, he was unsure how he should feel about his own intense attraction to her.

In an effort to break their connection, he side-stepped towards the bonfire. Makeshift benches encircled the fire a few feet away from where the logs and sticks were piled in the center. The air smelled thick with cedar and sweet pecans. Grant sat on a wooden plank that spanned two cut logs, and the thin board gave under his weight more than he was comfortable with.

"Can I join you?" Thandie said. "Everything is all set up over there and I can actually relax for a minute." She pointed to a blanket spread on the grassy area nearby. "Can I get you anything? Cider? Hotdog on a stick?"

"I have a filet waiting for me back in my cabin," he said. "Come sit with me." Though he considered the added weight on the board might bring them both down.

An owl hooted from a nearby tree, and a smile lifted Thandie's cheek. The firelight twinkled in her eyes and made her skin appear golden. She acquiesced and straddled the bench, facing toward his side. "I was afraid you wouldn't get it."

"I almost stepped right on the tray." He laughed.

"I knocked. You know?"

Grant was sure that he would have heard someone knocking on the door of his small accommodation. It was only one room and the bathroom. He snapped his fingers. "I must have been in the shower," he said. "Sorry I missed you."

Thandie leaned into his ear as he watched the flames bob and weave through the burning wood. "I missed you too."

At that sensual phrase, Grant turned his face. He was a breath away. "I thought we were keeping things professional." Her chest grazed his arm, and he froze, knowing that his next move was dangerous. If he did nothing, she might be insulted. If he closed the distance between them and let his lips warm hers, he was overstepping their professional host-guest relationship. Either way, he would lose.

Thank goodness for nosey-nellies, or in this case, nosey Margret. "Just kiss her already!" Margret encouraged and broke the crux of his impossible situation.

Thandie stood up and moved away without acknowledging Margret's jeering. Grant was relieved that the pressure was off of him, but annoyed that Thandie was now run-skipping up the short incline away from the heat.

"Wait! Thandie, wait up," Grant said and ran after her.

She was quick. Grant finally caught up to her, but only because she slowed down after reaching the refreshments area. White platters, arranged on top of stacked hay bales, reflected the fire's orange glow. Grant's mouth watered at the display of hotdogs and smore's ingredients in front of him. Beside the food, wheelbarrrows were piled high with woolen blankets and small lanterns. He made a mental note to include how cozy and welcoming the setup looked in his final report.

"You're fast," he said and braced his hands on his knees while he caught his breath. Though she faced away from him, he reached out for her hand. Removed from the other guests, Grant whispered her name, "Thandie."

"I can't," she said. "I didn't mean to insinuate. . ."

Her words trailed off, and Grant wrapped his arms around her shoulders. The fire licked the night sky. Flickers of embers floated through the air on the breeze around them like a wispy drape, giving them a sense of privacy from the other guests. Grant pulled her in, her back rested against his chest, and he spoke softly behind her ear. "I want to kiss you, but I'm more afraid than you know."

Her head rested back against his shoulder and her muscles relaxed into him. "Then tell me why this feels so natural," she said and turned to him. "I feel like I've known you for years. When we touch, I can't explain it. It's like the fire. Burning so bright and hot and . . . and . . ."

"And what? When this is all over—"

Her hand covered his mouth. "Whatever you are about to say, don't. We don't even know each other! And you don't want to say something you'll regret later."

"I know I won't," Grant said and bent his face to her. His mouth was just out of reach of her lips. Her breath cooled the edges of his mouth, and he lingered, waiting for her. She had to be the one to take the next step. It was no longer his impossible situation, it was hers.

His pulse thumped in his ears with excruciating impatience. The pitter-patter of his heart beat against his ribs. He sensed her coming closer. The slight arching up on her toes, the tension in her back, her chest rising with deep, thoughtful breaths, and her lips brushing ever so slightly against his.

"Rain," she sighed as their lips touched for too brief a second. She pulled away. "Rain. It's gonna rain soon. Can you smell that?"

Now she was toying with him, he suspected, as he looked to the sky and pointed past the orange glow. "Look, the stars are still out. There's no rain." He leaned in to pick back up where they left off, but the moment had unceremoniously passed by.

"It's not raining yet," she said. "It's coming. I'd check the radar, but there's virtually no signal around here. And, thanks to someone, I don't have a working phone anyway."

"You can use mine. I left it back in my room." Grant offered and realized that it may have sounded like he was making a move on her to get her in his cabin. So, to not leave any confusion between them, he added, "I can go get it really quick."

"I appreciate the offer, but we'll know here in about fifteen minutes, I suspect." Thandie bent down and came back up, holding two long metal skewers and two hotdogs. "Shall we?"

Grant took the dogs from her and threaded them on to the fork end of the skewers. "We better be quick about it," he teased.

"You just mark the time. I know what I know about this stuff."

At the fire, Thandie made an announcement that the rain would be coming soon and suggested that they wrap things up and head in for the night before it was too late. She sat on the bench and charred her hotdog, not taking the time to cook it properly.

She must have noticed him noticing her and laughed. "What? I like the skin all crunchy." She picked a slice off the hot dog and chewed it, and it did indeed crunch. "You like yours raw?"

Grant looked down and saw that his wasn't even in the fire, not enough to be cooked, or even warmed in the short time they had remaining before Thandie's rain might arrive. He stuck the dog directly in the fire and pulled it out a minute later, flame and all.

"That's better," she said and tapped her dog against his to put out the blaze. "Have you ever done this before?"

"What? Cooked a hotdog on a stick? Sure have," Grant said proudly with an anecdote at the ready about his time in the scouts, but she cut off his thought before he had a chance to tell his tale.

"No, I mean. Have you ever just gotten to know a woman, with no expectations, with no pressures from friends or family to move things along at a certain pace or in a certain way—"

"Or because it feels like if I don't get to know you that I'll be missing a piece of myself forever?" he said and immediately regretted being so frank. He hadn't even admitted to himself what was true. It was as though the years of running from love had brought him all the way around to a place where he might be able to experience it again. *Life is funny that way*, he thought and met her gaze.

She nodded with a grin and a bite of her lower lip on one side before taking another crunchy strip of hotdog and shoving it in her pretty mouth.

CHAPTER 17

Thandie laughed at how silly she was being with Grant. Their teasing had taken a sharp turn that evening onto a different road. Teasing had changed from friendly banter to a more suggestive, even sensual tit-for-tat that excited her and worried her at the same time. Since the wedding fiasco, she had been on a mission of self-discovery and healing, and not out hunting for another man who could ruin her life again.

She finished her thought as she finished chewing her bite of hotdog.

Although her blush was likely hidden in the light of the fire, she turned her face away from Grant. Had he really just said what he said? How could he feel such a strong emotion towards her? His words, *Missing a piece of myself forever*, rang in her mind.

His sentiment matched her own feelings. Which only begged the question: How was she feeling what she was feeling in the huge way she was feeling it? They were at ease with each other despite the tension that existed between them. There was nothing forced in the way they touched each other, looked at one another, or laughed together. The only thing that seemed forced was how they were both fighting it so much.

A current of excitement coursed through every nerve-ending in her body at the thought of seeing him or touching him in any way.

Now, having finished what remained of the hot dog, and with nothing standing in the way of her silence, she stood up from the log bench and stared into the fire. The flame's white tips tickled the few stars still peeking through the fast-moving clouds, and a plume of embers scattered into the air as the burned logs crumbled under their own weight.

"What is it?" Grant asked and stood beside her.

She saw herself in the bonfire. She had been like the wood at the bottom, being crushed by the mass of burning anger that she felt towards Davis. The resentment that she had carried for longer than she should have had nearly destroyed her. "This is ridiculous!"

A simple but apt statement.

She knew from his hesitation to speak that he didn't agree. If only he knew why she was so scared of getting hurt again. Never mind that her job, and the future of The Foundry was on the line if the week didn't go well. Getting involved with a guest was off the table, no matter how much she wanted to.

His hand grazed against hers. She wanted to take his hand, to feel his warm, strong fingers intertwine with hers. She wanted to stay up all night and talk with him until the sun came up. She wanted to see what he looked like in the last moments of night and the first light of dawn. She wanted . . .

"Grant. I need to tell you something."

"I know," he said. "I've known from the first day after the disastrous hike."

"You have? How?" she asked and rubbed her forehead.

"I overheard you talking to someone about it. And I want you to know that I understand completely."

Had she said something by accident? Did he know about Davis and the wedding that never was? Or was he the investor and thought she knew he was the spy? Did he mistake the personalized attention for something else altogether?

"I suppose it's better that you know now rather than later," she said, but she was still unsure what exactly he thought he knew. Now it just felt awkward to keep talking about it. Either he would feel foolish, or she would, and she couldn't bear another embarrassment.

"I'm glad we got that straight," he said, though her mind was more warped than ever. "Now can we stop pretending that this isn't happening between us and just have a nice time? Together?"

"I think that would be—" Thandie stopped and put her palms out in front of her. She caught the first few raindrops from the incoming shower. "Right on time." She didn't get to finish saying that she thought giving in to her attraction to him would be a terrible idea.

Above her, the sliver of moon disappeared behind the storm's leading edge. The stars twinkled in the distance to the east until they were mixed in with the glimmer of the falling rain in the firelight and obscured.

"I need to clean all this up really quick. You should go."

"Like I'm gonna leave you here by yourself," Grant said.

"It's my job. You're a guest here and I don't want you getting sick because of me," she said as the last couple left the bonfire and darted back to their cabin.

She scrambled and picked up the blankets, throwing them into the wheelbarrow beside the hay bales. No sooner did she gather the bins for the food than the sprinkling rain turned to a downpour.

In her periphery, Grant slid his plaid shirt off his shoulders and caused her to stop and stare. His white undershirt was immediately spotted with water droplets and clung to his skin. Grant pulled his plaid shirt up over his head like a makeshift umbrella and rushed to her side. She was helpless to do anything but watch the water sizzle off his toned body.

"Leave it. Let's get out of here," he said and held the shirt on one side while she took hold of the other.

Spreading the fabric to its widest breadth over their heads, they sprinted straight to his cabin, bypassing the walkway. His place was decidedly closer than hers was from the old shoreline, where the fire hissed its last breath behind them. Extending out from the side of his cabin and closest to them, they took shelter underneath a slanted carport roof, shivering from the cool air hitting their wet skin.

Grant wrapped his arms around her, and she took in as much of his warmth as he had to spare. "You're freezing, but I have an idea," he said. "I'll be right back." He placed his wet flannel shirt over her shoulders and disappeared into the dark around the back side of the cabin.

"Where are you going? Grant?" She was too cold to move and stood there. "Grant? Where are you?" Had he gone inside and not invited her? It was no matter, she would wait for a break in the rain and make a run for her cabin, soaked through. She rubbed her hands up and down her arms and watched as lights turned on and off in the various other guest houses. "Grant?" she whisper-yelled into the night.

"Over here," his voice called from behind the cabin.

She stepped around the corner toward his voice, curious at what she was walking into. She smiled and covered her mouth with the sleeve from his shirt as he came into view. "What are you doing?" She bit her lower lip but she was sure he could see the blush on her cheeks this time, despite the pale light.

He stood, waist deep and half-naked, in the round wooden hot tub. Steam rose like fog around him and seemed to melt away when it touched his toned skin, damp and glistening from the heat. His abs were impossibly chiseled, and he appeared dangerously tempting.

"Get in," he said from under the protection of a small gazebo roof that was only slightly wider than the spa below. His command wasn't an order, but an invitation. Though the way he spoke emphatically sent butterflies swarming to her chest.

No matter how enticing a dip in the spa sounded, she was certain joining him was against any professional rules. "I don't think I should. I'm at work right now."

"I thought we agreed to be done pretending," he said.

Technically they hadn't agreed to anything. She had never completed her thought out loud. But who was she kidding? Her reasons for not joining him were weakening by the millisecond. "I don't have a bathing suit?" her words came out like a question and not the strong reason she had intended them to be.

"Neither do I."

Her hands covered her face, and she shook her head as she contemplated what the heck she was about to do, and she knew she was about to do it from the way her feet were already moving towards him. "I think I should make a dash for it and go in for the night. The rain isn't too bad."

That excuse sounded worse than the other.

"Get in here." He chuckled. "You can worry about the rest tomorrow."

Thandie was lying to herself. The rain was bad. It was hard, stinging rain. The sort that is cold and sharp, like it may have been frozen rain when it was higher in the clouds and it had barely thawed out on its way to earth. Even so, joining him was crossing a line. Looking around at the otherwise quiet night, the guests had all turned in, the barn was dark, and the starry sky hid behind dark clouds. The coast was undeniably clear, and her resolve washed away with the rain.

She unbuttoned her jeans. *Breathe.* She slipped the zipper down so slowly, he likely thought she was teasing him when really she was second-guessing her ability to make good decisions.

Standing in the dim light, she knew he could see all of her. Heat pooled in her neck at the provocative scene she was partaking in. She crossed her arms at the hem of her shirt and peeled the wet tee from her torso and over her head. She hung it on one of a set of hooks fixed to the cabin's exterior wall. Under her tee she wore a white sports bra, which honestly covered more than a bikini top, but was a bra nonetheless. She kicked her boots off and slid her jeans down around her hips, over her bottom, and down her legs, and pulled one foot out at a time. She hung them on another hook under the porch roof.

"I hope I don't regret this," she said under her breath. She knew her boldness, independent of her lack of clothing, would shock him, and it did.

He stumbled, catching himself on one of the gazebo's supports. "Wow." Grant gasped. "Can I say that?"

She felt bolder than ever, finding power in her decision not to overthink what was happening. Thandie tiptoed across the half dozen flat concrete stepping stones that led from the carport to the back patio. Wasting no time and dodging the fat raindrops, she climbed the riser and stepped into the hot tub. The whole scene seemed too good to be true, even for her. A spa heated by fire, the rain pattering against the wooden gazebo shingles, her, in only her white bra and panties, and the man who she had only known for three days holding his hand out for her to take.

She hesitated, remembering her promise to herself that she didn't need a man. But for the first time in longer than she could recall, she felt that perhaps needing help and accepting help could be two different things. With Grant's assistance, Thandie sunk down into the warm water and let it envelop her cold muscles like a hug.

"This feels good," she said.

"See?" Grant lowered himself down into the water across from her. "I told you I had a good idea."

She let her head fall back to the rim of the spa and relaxed her chest and shoulders. "It was a good idea." A sigh whistled through her lips.

They sat in silence for several minutes, sharing glances and blushes that she was certain were on her cheeks. Her knees touched his in the small space, and she didn't flinch to move away. His arms rested on the rim above the waterline, and he closed his eyes, relaxing into the curved back rest.

They didn't even need to talk. The rain poured and splattered in the mud around them, which she knew meant that there was going to be a ton of clean up in the morning. The Foundry grounds would be swampy in areas already soaked from the previous rain. But right now, she was content to just sit in the spa and enjoy the serenity. She wouldn't have admitted only a couple of days earlier that she needed this.

"Tell me, Thandie," he said while his eyes remained shut. "Did you always want to be a camp counselor?"

The title wasn't exactly right, and she thought to let it slide, but didn't. "Activities director, and no. I sort of fell into this job."

Grant opened one eye just long enough to catch hers and closed it again. "How long have you been in the business?"

"Four days."

At this answer, his lids flew open, and he leaned forward, closing the distance between them. He searched her face. "Oh." A giggle. "You're serious."

"As a dead horse. Is that bad to admit?"

Having leaned forward, his hands now rested on her knees under the water. His touch sent a shock up her neck to where it landed behind her ears. "I would never have known. You are very good at your job." She must have shifted her legs slightly, and he became aware of the intimate way he was touching her. He sat back away from her, repositioning his hands above the water line again on the rim of the spa. "You may be too good at your job."

Now she thought perhaps he was the spy after all, in which case she should definitely not be in the hot tub with him. However, there was no other evidence that he worked for the investor, and her money was still on the bubbly Daisy and her Mr. Brent. "How do you mean, *I'm too good?*"

"For starters, you show the guests way too much personalized attention. There's no way you can keep up that level of care. You'll burn out."

Of course, he didn't know that she and the rest of the staff were putting on the very best show they could for whoever the snoop was. "I appreciate the compliment, and the concern. But I assure you that I won't get burned out from doing my job well. Believe it or not, I am having a fantastic time as camp counselor, as you call it."

"Yes, but you're in this job for a few days. What happens after a year, or even five years? Will you like it then?"

"That sounds like a question for you, not me." Thandie sensed an exhaustion in him, but if she pushed him to tell her why he was really there, the game would be up. "You don't need to talk about it—"

"I want to," he said and nodded. His grin melted any objections or deflections she had prepared. "I travel all the time for work."

"And you like to travel?"

He shifted in the spa and pulled one leg up so that his ankle rested on the other knee, leaving half his leg sticking out of the water. His hands wrapped around the exposed skin, and he leaned forward. He looked serious, nervous, or cold, though it was likely not the latter, given their current whereabouts.

"I do. Like to travel, that is. But lately, the thought of going home, sleeping in the same bed, and having someone to talk to who really knows me has been creeping into my mind more and more."

"You could get a cat?"

"And who would take care of said cat when I'm gone for weeks and months at a time?"

"If you hate it, then quit," she joked, but the look on his face was not an amused one. She had hit a nerve.

"You know, sometimes you go down a path in life where there aren't any exit ramps. The money is good. And I do love seeing the world and experiencing so many different people and cultures. It's just—" he paused and looked out into the rain past her.

"It's just you want to jump the curb and get off anywhere you can. I get that." Thandie leaned in and placed her hands on top of his. "That's how I ended up here. I jumped the curb a few months ago and have been off-roading ever since. Trying to find a new way."

"And it's going well?"

"Gosh no. I've been scared more times than I like to admit. I'm out of money and out of options. So, for the time being, this job is all I have."

"What has you running so hard?" he asked with no judgment in his voice. His regard for her was like an embrace that she didn't want to let go of.

"I wasted a lot of time being something for someone else instead of being anything for me."

His eyes turned dark and pierced hers with an intensity of a lion. Her breath caught at his dramatic shift. "Who hurt you?"

"You don't even know who or what I'm—"

"It was that Davis person. The one you stacked stones for and kicked, rather impressively I'd like to point out, into the field. If I ever find him, I'll beat his a—"

"You will not." Thandie took his hands from pantomiming a fistfight in the air in front of her and squeezed them in hers. "I don't need anyone to fight my battles for me. Plus, I let all of that go today. I realized that I am not *his* mistakes. I can make plenty of my own. I shouldn't need to carry his too."

Grant pulled his hands away and took her by the waist. Her muscles flexed under his grasp as he pulled her closer. "Is this a mistake?" His voice was soft like a whisper, but with the rasp of a man that knew what he wanted.

"Probably," she whispered back as their lips met.

Grant didn't take more than she offered. Even in the way he held back his power, she recognized a tenderness, a caring, and a love inside of him.

Needing air, Thandie pulled away. "What are you running from, Grant Goldie, and why The Foundry?"

"You want the truth?"

She nodded.

"I lost someone whom I loved—"

"I'm so sorry. You don't have to tell me more if you don't want to," Thandie said. Even if Grant wanted to say more, she didn't know if she had the capacity to show as much empathy as would be appropriate. She was tired, and very distracted by the fact that they were sitting together so intimately and exposed.

He paused, considering her words, but did not finish his story. He nodded ever so slightly, as though to say it was ok. That he was okay.

"I should go." The rain had let up sometime during their conversation, and she needed to get away from him before real mistakes were made. She stepped out of the spa and grabbed her wet clothes. There was no point in putting them on her soaking body. "I'll see you tomorrow," she said as she disappeared into the safety of the dark night.

CHAPTER 18

The next morning, Grant was more confused than ever about what he was doing with his life. During his conversation with Thandie last night, he had accidentally admitted the truth about just how exhausted he was. After he became a widower, his job had given him purpose and a sense of control over his life. Moreover, his job had been a well-timed distraction.

Thandie, or perhaps the serene setting of The Foundry itself, showed him that he couldn't go on like that forever. Ringing in his head and heart was the warning that he had given to the incredible woman sitting in the spa with him last night. *What happens after a year, or even five? You'll burn out.* He was burned out. He knew that now, and maybe he was ready for a change.

The thought of settling down was a secret he had kept in the back of his mind. Until last night, he hadn't been brave enough to even say it out loud to himself, let alone to a spirited woman who he barely knew. But being around her felt so easy. Why had he broken his own rule to not get involved with the people or places he visited?

"Because I'm an idiot," he said and buried his head under his bed pillow.

There was nothing wrong with a little flirting. Since there was little pressure that he would ever see her again, it seemed harmless enough. But Thandie was different. He not only wanted to see her again, and soon if he could help it, but he wanted to see much, much more of her.

For once, he wasn't being consumed by his own heartache. Instead, he possessed an intense focus on what or whom had wounded Thandie and sent her on an escape mission. A mission that had landed her in the boonies, running a wellness retreat, and catering to a bunch of middle-aged people. She alluded to the cause of her pain, but she wasn't in any more of a hurry to spill all her guts than he was. And who could blame her? They each hardly knew the other.

Grant threw his pillow against the wall and flopped back. Staring at the rounded beams of the ceiling, he remembered the curves of her body as she had slipped out of her clothing and into the warm spa water. Her tan skin contrasting in the low light with her white bra and panties that looked more like a bikini than underwear, and her wet hair falling in long strands over her shoulders. And one delicious brown curl that clung to the damp skin of her chest. How he wished to explore the depths . . . *of her soul.*

He shot up from the bed and straightened the covers. "What are you doing, Grant Goldie?" he scolded himself. "You're being selfish. And stupid. And—" He had nothing more to chastise himself about. He had spent a decade wallowing in the cage he constructed around his own heart. She was the one that needed healing now, not him. She was the one who showed him there was hope. She was the one that he couldn't stop thinking about. She was the one—

The landline phone rang in the kitchen.

Grant dropped the throw pillows where he stood and hurried across the room. "Go for Grant," he said and pressed the handset to his ear.

"Grant. Davis Mothan here, I'm glad I caught you. I tried your cell first, but it wouldn't connect. The front desk put me through."

Just hearing the name *Davis* sent a twinge through his shoulders. "Sorry about that. The signal here is terrible, but I have it on good authority that the issue is being remedied." Grant took a deep breath and sat in one of the leather chairs beside the front door. "What can I do for you, Mr. Mothan?"

"I was hoping for an update. And call me Davis, please."

The way his boss said *Davis*, holding out the *s* like a simpering snake, curled Grant's stomach. And his fist. He knew there was no way that Mr. Mothan was the same man who had hurt Thandie, but the name alone caused a protective tension to ignite his sinew.

"Things are going really well. I don't have my final report completed, obviously, but my first impression is a good one. This place is spectacularly beautiful and serene. The food is fantastic. The activities are engaging and unique. The director is amazing. Thandie has a way with the guests that I've never seen before." Grant paused as Thandie walked by his window on the pathway outside. He swallowed hard. "She makes everyone feel like they are the most important person at the retreat. It feels like home here."

"Sounds like you want to move in." Davis chuckled again in that haughty, not funny way. The same way Davis had sounded when he spoke of the people busying themselves on the streets below his corner office. "What did you say the director's name was again?"

Only half paying attention to the man on the line, Grant answered, "Thandie. She's doing a bang-up job." Grant craned his neck, and his eyes followed the sway of her hips as she carried a large tub of something towards the dock. He would be joining the next activity at the bottom of the hour. "Anyway, I have some more things to investigate before I'll be ready to give my full opinion. For one thing, it's very wet here, and I see a potential issue during certain times of the year when profitability might go down."

"And other times?"

"As long as there are procedures in place so that the guests still experience what they've paid for, then it should be fine. I can tell you that your investment would allow them to hire more staff and improve some of the buildings where inclement weather activities could be held. But overall, you might want to start looking for your checkbook."

"I'm very keen on moving forward, but I'll wait for your full report. And Grant, don't let this woman—the activities director you said—blind you with her charisma and beauty." Davis coughed away from the receiver and cleared his throat. "I'll be in touch."

The line went dead, and Grant shook his head at the awkward goodbye. He hadn't mentioned Thandie's beauty, or her charisma, yet Davis had. Was Grant's crush on her so obvious that even a person thousands of miles away could tell how smitten he was, or was Davis more informed about The Foundry and its staff than he had first let on?

Checking the time, Grant slipped on his hiking boots and tucked the red laces inside the tongue. He was in a hurry to catch up to the woman who had captured his attention. Though there wasn't much catching up to do. Thandie had stopped twenty paces down the path and was bent over picking up the numerous scissors and pruning shears that lay scattered on the ground. The tub lay nearby and was turned onto one side where she must have dropped it.

"Thandie!" he called out. "Thandie."

She removed an earbud from one ear and looked over her shoulder at him. A smile lit her face as their eyes met. He knew he was smiling too. He couldn't help himself. Slowing, the damp gravel shifted beneath his feet as he met up with her.

"What can I do for you, Mr. Goldie?" she said. Her smile had betrayed her at first, but was replaced with a soft and distant look in her eyes.

"Mr. Goldie, huh? Okay? Can I help you out here?"

"I appreciate the offer, but I'm nearly finished. Have you eaten today?" she asked. "Brunch is being served in the barn. God, that sounds so terrible. *In the barn*," she said with an affected country accent.

"You don't like *the barn?*" he said and chuckled at the way he had mimicked her country voice.

"I've been trying to come up with different names for it. The clubhouse. The main house. The hall. Nothing sounds right. But the barn sounds too basic."

"It is what it is. If you tell someone to go to the barn, they'll know exactly where to head to."

"True," she admitted as she rocked her head back and forth. "It doesn't leave any room for misinterpretation."

She seemed distracted by something, constantly looking over his shoulder and around at anything other than him. "Is everything all right?" Grant asked.

Thandie laughed her answer. "Of course. Why would you think anything is wrong?"

"We said no pretending, right?"

She shrugged and laughed out her response again. "I'm not pretending. I'm totally fine. Everything is fine. You?"

There was no use in fighting her on the detail at the moment. He knew she was bothered by something, and most likely by the something they had shared while in the spa last night. He suspected she was self-conscious about having let her guard down with him. He wasn't embarrassed by it at all. He had felt freedom in her honesty. He had felt something natural and real for the first time in a long time. And the cracks in the wall protecting his heart were deepening with each additional moment he spent near her.

"I'll let you get back to it," he said. "The nature walk is soon?"

"Yes. I'll see you there?"

He nodded and turned back towards the cabin. That freedom he had felt with her was so much more than just a conversation with a beautiful woman. The part he focused on was that he had *felt*. All the years of taking on every job he could to get away from dealing with the realities of his life, he had been hurting, too. That feeling of wanting to settle down, of wanting to have a life with someone again, meant he was healing. It meant that his feelings for Thandie weren't just about her. His feelings meant that he was ready to move on. It meant that things were about to change in his life.

And change for the better.

CHAPTER 19

From where she stood at the old shoreline, Thandie looked over the heads of the guests about a thousand times to see if Grant was going to join them for the nature walk. After brunch was cleaned up, they had all gathered in the barn to walk down together, but Grant didn't show.

Perhaps he'll run me over again, she thought with a giggle.

Thandie had been looking forward to this activity since she first conceived of it all of five days ago. Botany was her passion, and she finally had a chance to use her skills properly. Squatting down to the ground, she moved some long grass away from a tuft of small purple flowers that hugged the rich soil. "Come look at these," she said to the group.

"What are we looking at here?" Daisy asked in a spry tone, and crouched beside Thandie. "These are the prettiest little flowers, aren't they Brent?" Brent grunted in agreement.

"These are called Vinca, or Common Periwinkles. It's an invasive species in North America, but aren't they pretty? They bloom here for most of the year, and they even have medicinal uses," Thandie said and picked a small bloom. She tucked the flower behind Daisy's ear and winked. "Just don't eat it. Unlike other flowers that are edible, this one will make you sick."

Daisy stood and showed off her pretty prize. "Like it?" Brent nodded and gave her a quick kiss on one cheek.

"How do you know about all this stuff?" Anne asked and picked a periwinkle for her own hair.

"I'm a botanist." No further explanation was needed.

Before heading out of view of the barn, Thandie scanned the pathways for any sign of Grant. Once they continued down the old shoreline, it would be hard for him to catch up or find them. But the path was deserted. Though her shoulders slumped with disappointment at his absence, part of her was relieved she would have more time to process her feelings before seeing him again. She knew they would need to talk about the kiss and her unexpected attraction towards him, but she had been too tired after returning to her cabin to stay awake and think on it. Once morning came and she began prepping for the nature walk, she was too busy to think about the way his warm lips had hugged hers so.

Seeing no one, they headed south, and she continued pointing out what she knew of the native northeast plants, insects, and birds. Luckily, with all the rain, the countryside was teeming with interesting things to speak on.

A dashing robin flaunted his slate-blue wings and rusty underbelly as it darted along the ground in front of her, and grasshoppers soared above the swaying grasses in the wilds along the trail. As she was never out of facts, Thandie used her keen sense of her surroundings and drew attention to anything she felt the others might find stimulating.

She paused. "Everyone, take out your binoculars and focus them just below the pines there. You'll see a group of deer."

The weather could not have been better for the activity. *The best weather by far this week,* she thought. The temperature was in the mid-sixties and a steady, gentle breeze spread fragrant fresh air around the property. A jumble of little white and yellow butterflies pollinated flowers and fluttered from plant to plant, glowing brightly in the late morning sun.

"Thandie," Margret said. "Would you be a dear and help me with these? I believe they're broken."

"The binoculars are not broken! You are. Now, give them here," Anne said and wrenched the small black binoculars from Margret's hands before Thandie could get to them. Anne turned the binoculars around and rotated the dial all the way to the other side. "Try it again."

Margret looked through the lenses and smiled. "Well, I'll be."

"I mean, honestly, woman. I don't know how you survived so long without me in your life," Anne said.

"The deer are so cute," Daisy proclaimed and pointed across the way. "Can we pet them?" she asked and turned to Thandie, who shook her head no.

Up ahead, the pathway split in two directions. To the right, it dipped down around a rocky outcropping. To the left, the trail narrowed and cut between a steep hillside and the stone ledge. She stopped at the fork and assessed the safety of both directions before sending any of the guests through. As it was her first time walking this trail, she couldn't afford to take a chance on someone getting hurt.

Determining the path to her right was clear of overgrowth, she began directing the guests around the large rocks. Daisy and Brent, who had participated in all the activities so far and were the leading candidate for being the investor's scouts, led the way. Margret and Anne rounded the rock edge next, followed by the rekindled lovers, Clara and William. The trio of older women had again missed this activity, which Thandie was now suspecting had to do little with the weather and more to do with where or when the food was being served at the various events. Buzz and his daughter, Frances, had gone into town for something, but said they would join them for supper. Fish-and-chips, last she heard.

As William went last, Thandie heard a "Psst" coming from the path to the left, the path that went between the hillside and the rocks. The path that none of the others had gone down. She took a few steps in the direction of the call and listened again.

The group had gone through and were waiting at the bottom of a small decline, and she looked back at the way they had come from. But seeing and hearing nothing, she stepped back around the front side of the stone ledge.

Another "Psst" came from the same direction as before.

Thandie, wanting to prove that she wasn't hearing things, walked the more dangerous route around the hillside. Between the walls of rock, Grant appeared with a wild grin. His excited eyes sent her heart racing. He had the look of a mischievous boy up to no good. From behind his back, he pulled out a bundle of yellow flowers. The scraggly ends were uneven as though he'd picked the stems with his hands and not cut them cleanly.

"What do you have there?" she asked and joined him in the privacy of the narrow cut-through.

He presented the flowers to her, and she gasped in shock.

"Here," he said and pushed the bouquet towards her again. "I thought you may like these. They glow in the sunlight and—"

Thandie swatted the bouquet of wildflowers from his hand and took his arm, holding it straight out so that he could see the numerous swelling red bumps popping up on his skin. "There's poison ivy in there. When did you pick those?"

"A couple hours ago. Why?" he said.

"It looks like you're already having an allergic reaction."

"No, I can't be."

"It'll be fine," Thandie said while shifting her head to try and meet his distant gaze. "Just about everyone I grew up with had a run-in with the stuff at one time or another."

"I just wanted to give you something you would like." Grant

extended his arm out as he pointed to the flowers scattered on the ground. His eyes widened when he saw the extent of the bulging bumps on his arm. "Oh no." Color left his face, and he stumbled to the side.

Thandie reached out for him and caught him by the shirt hem. She rested his back against the rockface as his breathing became rough and uneven. His reaction looked less like an allergy and more like a panic attack. She was unsure exactly what was happening, but she knew he needed help.

"Grant, look at me." His teary eyes found hers and his breathing slowed as he matched her example. "Let me help you back to the barn."

"Am I going to die? Are you going to bury me right here? You can put those flowers on my grave. It's fitting, don't you think?" His delirious phrases ran together.

"Don't talk like that," she said as her concern turned to fear. Not only did he require help, so did she, and she wasn't afraid to ask for it, for once. She yelled for help and began walking him back up the trail.

William and Clara joined her after only a couple of pleas. "Clara, will you lead the others back to the barn? And Will, can you help me with Grant?" The couple helped without hesitation, and Thandie was glad for the assistance.

"What happened?" William asked as he hoisted Grant's arm over his own shoulder.

"I think he's having an allergic reaction to some poison ivy." Thandie took her canteen and popped the lid off. She handed it to Grant, who took it and brought it up to his lips. "Drink," she ordered.

Grant's steps slowed, and he caught her gaze. "I could have killed you with those flowers. And I was trying to be nice," he moaned between weeping and laughing.

"Drink," she said again and pushed the canteen to his lips.

She knew he was having an emotional reaction along with the

physical, and he jabbered nonsense all the way up the hill. Leo met them halfway down the driveway in front of the barn and took Grant's other arm from Thandie. "He's having an allergic reaction. And a panic attack. Will you get him inside and have him lie down?"

Thandie took off in a full sprint toward the office where the bin of first aid supplies was located. Glad that she had noticed it on an earlier trip to the loft, she rifled through and found the bottle of allergy medicine and cream. Meeting the men downstairs in the *cucina*, she kneeled beside Grant where he was lying on the floor.

"I need you to take this pill," she said and sat him up a little.

"I don't like sushi," he coughed out and brushed her hand away.

The little white pill flew across the floor, and she took another one. "It's not sushi. It's medicine to help you feel better. Now, open up." Thandie placed the pill on his tongue and held the canteen to his lips. She tilted the container until the water dripped out and into his mouth. His breath smelled of cinnamon, and she guessed that he had recently brushed his teeth. She grinned at the thought of how the situation could have gone quite differently had he not picked the ivy by accident. Her racing pulse could have had a more enjoyable catalyst.

"Should I call the doctor?" Leo asked.

"I don't think it's necessary. He's not anaphylactic." She pulled up Grant's sleeve and exposed angry-looking bumps on his forearm. "This is typical contact dermatitis. I think his mental reaction is just shock. He was totally fine, other than his skin, until he saw his arm looking like this."

William returned with damp paper towels and a small trashcan. "Here, wash the area and throw those away after." He handed over the items and added, "I was a boy scout and I've seen this before. He'll be okay."

"Thanks, William," Leo said. "You should go wash up since you touched him and maybe were exposed too."

"Right," William said. "You got this?"

Leo nodded and William departed. "Where are the others?" Leo asked Thandie as she cleaned Grant's arm and hands.

"Clara is leading them back here."

"A golf cart would be nice right about now." Leo attempted levity, but she wasn't in the mood to laugh. "I'll go check on things."

"Go," she said and kept her attention trained on Grant.

The color was returning to his cheeks, and his eyes looked at her instead of through her as they had since his reaction began. She helped him sit up and leaned him against the wall under the *Cucina* sign. Thandie inquired with her eyes whether he was ok, and he nodded ever so slightly. She finished cleaning all the reddened skin that she could see, but the spots extended underneath the edge of his rolled sleeve.

"Can I take your shirt off?" she asked, but was already unbuttoning his mushroom-colored oxford. He didn't protest as her hands moved under the collar's front edge and along his collarbones. His biceps flexed under her touch and sent heat into her cheeks. Being careful not to scratch his arms, Thandie pulled each sleeve down over his hands and tossed his shirt aside. Underneath, Grant's tight white tee-shirt hugged his chest and abs. It was too bad she had no excuse to take that layer off, also.

The rash creeped up Grant's arm just beyond the crook of his elbow, where it had settled the worst. She cleaned the area as gently as she could, though he hissed in through his teeth several times. "Sorry," she said and pressed a clean, damp paper towel on the bumps. "You should probably take a cool shower. And then put some itch cream on this. Do you need a doctor?"

"I need you," he slurred and laid his head back against the wall.

"You do?" she whispered in disbelief and assumed he had misspoke. *More delirium*, she thought.

She'd seen skin reactions like his before when she grew up living in the country. Farmers were always getting stung or bitten by something. He would be fine, she knew it, but he would be exhausted from the rush of adrenaline wreaking havoc on his system.

"Should I help you back to your cabin?"

She knew what his answer would be, and she wanted him to say it.

"That would be nice. Thank you, Thandie."

"It's my pleasure."

"It's your job," he reminded her as he stood.

There it was. The tit-for-tat that she had grown to love participating in very much. Seeing him near passing out, and in obvious distress, had left her feeling utterly ridiculous for having questioned her feelings for him earlier that day. She had been afraid to talk to him about the kiss. *A kiss! It's not like he proposed or something*, she thought.

It was evident now, more than ever, that she liked this man very much. But their timing could not be any worse.

At that thought, thunder splintered across the old lake, carrying a tempest on its back. Thick clouds darkened the sky outside the barn and replaced the bright, clean air with an ominous green hue. She needed to get Grant to his cabin before the skies opened up. There was no way she was getting stuck out in another downpour.

Standing, Thandie crossed her wrists out in front and took each of Grant's hands in hers. "There's a storm coming." She braced one leg in front and one in back and pulled him upright. "We need to go."

More thunder rumbled low across the shallow valley. The delicate crystals of the chandelier shook above their heads, and a blinding light filled the space for a split second. She didn't have time to close her eyes or shutter her ears to the booming sound. Before things got any worse, Thandie took Grant's arm, and they made their way outside.

In the meantime, Leo had intercepted the guests and was directing them back to their own cabins. Everyone except for Margret and Anne, who were coming up the path towards the barn and aiming for Thandie and Grant.

Margret jogged ahead. "Is he well?"

Thandie nodded. "He will be. But I need to get him inside before the storm hits. I should be up to the barn in a little while. I hear the chef is preparing a traditional fish-and-chips tonight."

"What a treat," Margret said with excitement sparking between her clapping fingers.

"Get inside while you can," Thandie said.

"I agree, ladies," Leo chimed in. "Get indoors."

Thandie and Grant continued to his cabin, passing her own on the way. She thought to stop by and grab her coat, because she hadn't needed one until now, but the thunder cracking overhead had them moving with urgency towards the Bear Cabin. Grant's cabin. Sometime between periwinkles and poison ivy, the weather had turned, though she hadn't noticed with all the commotion. As though the pressure for her to put on a fantastic week for The Foundry wasn't enough, she highly suspected that the weather was purposefully throwing a wrench in her activity plans.

CHAPTER 20

Inside Grant's cabin, Thandie left him sitting in the kitchen while she turned on the shower for him. "I don't want you touching anything until you clean your skin off."

"And yours," he said while she was still in the bathroom checking the water temperature.

She looked down at her hands and forearms. Small red dots had popped up from where she had touched Grant and when she had swatted the flowers from his grip. She didn't even realize that she had been affected until he mentioned it just now.

"You go first," he said.

"Here? No, that's okay." She shook the warm water drops from her hands and went out to the kitchen. "I'll go back to my place. I can come check on you later."

"Absolutely not." There was no amount of negotiating room in his voice. "You heard the storm coming. You should hop in really quick, and then I'll go."

She protested again, but he was right. The longer she stayed there stalling, the closer the storm was getting. "Do you have something I can put on?" She showed him her arms. "My clothes are probably covered too."

"Of course. There's a pair of robes hanging behind the bathroom door. I used the gray one, but the white one hasn't been touched. You're more than welcome to borrow it." Grant shooed her away with his hand.

After she got cleaned up, she wrapped the fluffy white robe around her body and tied the rope closure as tight as she could comfortably stand. She used her claw clip to brush out her half curly, half straight hair, and pinched her cheeks for a bit of color. A deep breath was necessary, and she took three. Steam escaped the bathroom when she finally opened the door, and she felt like she was in a made-for-TV movie about a ghost haunting a Roman bath.

Grant hadn't moved from his place in the kitchen, and his smile melted her heart and her nerves. "Your turn," she said as another crack of thunder shook the old windows. "Better hurry."

As he turned the shower water back on, Thandie grabbed an empty trash bag from under the sink and opened it. "Since you're not cleaned off yet, can you grab my clothes and put them in here?" She held the flimsy white plastic bag open, careful not to be touched by the contaminated garments as he slid them inside. "Now take yours off," she said.

He pointed to himself, and she nodded.

His button-down shirt was already sitting somewhere on the floor at the barn and his white tee left little to Thandie's imagination. Even so, her pulse quickened, and her neck muscles tightened behind her ears. He grinned on one side and took hold of the tee's hem. Grant shimmied the shirt slowly up his torso, teasing her with every inch of exposed skin. The worst part was that he knew what he was doing to her, and she knew that he knew, and liked him for it all the more.

She bit her bottom lip, not because she was incredibly hungry for him, but as an effort to hide the broad smile that was pulling at her cheeks. Grant threw his shirt like a basketball, and she caught it in the bag. She turned away, knowing his cargos were next to come off.

Grant was having far too much fun with this game, and she was about to lose herself in the valleys of his amazing abs if she looked any longer. *Yes, turning away from him was the best thing to do*, she thought. "Let me know when you're done taking those off."

"All done," he said, and she could tell he was smiling.

Thandie kept her eyes shut tightly and moved toward the sound of his voice echoing off the tile in the bathroom. She held the bag open and felt the weight of his remaining clothes fall in. She backed out, careful of the moist floor beneath her feet, and felt for the door handle. Only after the latch clicked did she open her eyes again.

"You're cute, you know," he said from the other side of the door.

"You're covered with poison, you know."

She could hear him laughing as the sound of the shower changed from hitting the pan to hitting his skin. Outside, rain began to fall. Soft at first, and then hard, like marbles hitting the roof. The downpour drowned out the sounds from the bathroom altogether, but not the sound of her heart beating against her ribs.

Tying the bag and washing her hands in the sink, a drip of water hit the tip of her nose. Looking at the ceiling peak, she saw another drop. And another. She didn't want to spend one more minute being wet, or covered with mud, but if the dripping kept up, they would soon be in a bath. She grabbed a mixing bowl from the kitchen and placed it on the floor below the dripping ceiling just as she heard another drop splash into the kitchen sink. *Lucky*, she thought.

It was obvious the place needed work. Not just Grant's cabin, but The Foundry as a whole. Leo and America had made their funds stretch farther than the money probably should have, and the barn itself was a stunning spectacle, but the funds could be used for things like roof repair and additional staff. No amount of perfectly planned activities would make up for a guest waking up to a soggy bed or a wet kitchen.

Grant came out of the bathroom like a zombie wearing a gray robe, not unlike the color that his face had turned after seeing the rash earlier. His skin had all the peachy color back in it now, but his eyes were vacant, and his shoulders slumped forward. Making straight for the bed without even looking at her, he flopped in and said, "I feel awful."

"I'm not surprised. It's probably the allergy medicine making you feel drowsy. But look," she said and pointed at his wrist, "it's working."

He turned his hand over and back again before collapsing into the pillows piled in front of the whitewashed headboard.

"You were in quite a state of shock at the sight of the rash. Now that the adrenaline is wearing off, and you're all cleaned up, you should sleep."

"Are you staying?" he asked. His eyes were closed. "I want you to."

"I shouldn't. But I don't have a choice right now."

His eyes flew open at that moment, though she wasn't sure if he was responding to what she said about staying, or because of the lightning and peals of thunder outside. The clap was so loud it drowned out the rain pounding on the roof. "I can't sleep under these conditions," he said. "The thunder . . . My mind's racing and replaying what happened, and you . . ." His eyes drank her in. "You, looking like that."

She looked down at herself, wrapped in the robe, and shook her head at him. "Try to sleep," she said and pointed at the dripping ceiling with the bowl positioned underneath. "And I'll keep an eye on this."

"Let's hope that doesn't get worse," Grant said and took a

calming breath in. "I'm actually feeling better knowing you're staying with me for now."

His sentiment was sweet, but she hoped the rain would let up soon. The longer she stayed with Grant, alone in his cabin, and wearing only a robe, the less willpower she would have to not accidentally kiss the man again. "I can call Leo. Maybe there's something he can do about the roof. Though I doubt it while it's still raining."

"No need. I can fix this," he said and hopped up with all the confidence of a boy wearing a cape—in this case, a robe with a rope belt that he was twirling in the air like a lasso—and walked to the kitchen.

"What are you doing? Sit back down!" Thandie said and reached out to intercept him. "You can't possibly fix a roof—"

"I didn't say I was fixing the roof." His smirk weakened any resolve that she had left, and she fell to the edge of the bed where Grant had just been. He returned from the kitchen with a split of red wine in one hand and two stemmed glasses hanging from his other and held them up like a man presenting his big catch.

"This is your idea of a fix?" she said and took the bottle from him. "You should drink water, not wine."

Thandie took the bottle back to the kitchen and filled a glass from the tap for him. He took it, reluctantly, and drank the whole thing to appease her, probably in hopes of getting wine next. She handed him the bottle, partly to see what he would do, and partly because she could use a glass of wine too.

"Pour," she said.

He opened the bottle and poured an inch into the wineglass.

"I'm really sorry," Thandie said.

He swirled the rich liquid and held the glass out for her. "Sorry for what?"

"This week has been a total disaster. You were supposed to have a perfect week and all it's done is rain and rain."

"I don't see it that way. Here." He released the glass into her possession, and she took a sip. "I have had a very nice, albeit unexpected, time so far this week. I've biked, and hiked, and stretched, and breathed, and stacked, and soaked, and—"

"Nearly died."

Grant scooted next to her on the edge of the bed and placed his hand on her robe-covered knee. "Thandie, look at me. I did not nearly die. I overreacted—"

"Panicked?"

"Yes, panicked, when I thought I was having an allergic reaction. But I'm fine now."

"You didn't look fine, Grant. I was really worried," Thandie said.

Grant swallowed hard and shifted his eyes to the ceiling and back to her. "I'm sorry I frightened you in that way. Believe me, it was not my intention," he said with a nervous chuckle through his nose. "You know, I picked flowers for you because I like you very much and I wanted to make you feel special. You've spent the last few days making me, and everyone else here, feel that way. And I wanted to say thank you. What happened was in no way your fault. Nor is all the rain."

"But—"

He put his finger over her lips. "But nothing. You have done your absolute best with what you had to work with. I think you'll get a fantastic report after this. I mean, all the guests will give wonderful reviews. I know I will."

Had he really just said he would give a good report? Thandie thought. *Grant Goldie was the investor's scout?* She didn't want to believe it. She was sure it was Daisy and her partner, who seemed to want nothing to do with being there at first. She couldn't just come out and ask him and risk him thinking she was acting out of self-interest for her job and The Foundry. Even if he wasn't the spy, it changed nothing about how she felt in that moment. His hand resting heavy on her knee, his warmth radiating off of him . . .

Grant's comment had been nothing more than a man attempting to console a friend.

"You really think it's been a good week so far?"

"I do."

The way he said those words undid her.

His were the same words she had repeated and practiced out loud before her ill-fated wedding. The words she had imagined Davis saying to her, only now, it wasn't Davis standing in front of her at the altar in her mind. This strong man, who made her laugh, and pushed her buttons, who was kind and caring and ridiculous, had replaced Davis in the image. Grant was standing before her, in a blue suit, with a yellow flower on his lapel, and smiling, with glistening eyes and rosy lips.

"What is it?" he asked and ripped her from her daydream.

"Nothing, I was just thinking about . . ." She couldn't tell him the truth; it would frighten him. She drank some more wine. And more, finishing off the portion that he had poured. She reached across him for the bottle and proceeded to refill her own. Handing him the small bottle, exhausted of its contents, she raised her glass. "To a new friendship, and mostly dry cabins to hunker down in."

He raised his empty glass and clinked it against hers as thunder boomed and shook the cabin. She flinched, nearly losing control of her drink, but he caught her against his body while steadying her hand that held the wineglass. As he guided her hand towards the end table, the lights flickered off.

She was in no hurry to remove herself from him, but he popped up and left her falling onto the mattress. Across the room, Grant clicked the lighter a few times at the fireplace, and the timber logs caught flame.

"You want something to eat?" he asked, but didn't wait for her answer. Grant retrieved the plate she had left for him the night before from the fridge. In the glow of the fire, Grant cut up pieces of cold steak and skewered a bit on the end of a long fork.

Repeating the action again, he handed the second one to her before grabbing another bottle of wine. "Now it's a proper meal."

"This is absurd. We're eating leftover steak off of a stick, drinking too much red wine, sitting by a fire because the power is out, and the cabin might just fill up with rainwater before morning. This is not a proper meal."

Grant took her skewer and handed her a glass back. "Drink."

She did.

The firelight danced in his eyes and reflected the truth to her. It was the most perfect meal she had ever had with him. With anyone. She leaned toward him slowly, testing his reaction to her proximity. If their previous encounters were any indication, he would respond in kind. And he did.

Their lips met. His warm, supple skin, tasting of wine, pressed into her with small rhythmic movements. His hand came around the back of her neck and cradled it the way he had during their first encounter rolling in the mud. A throaty sigh escaped her as she melted into his embrace and wrapped her free arm around his shoulders. For a moment, it was as though every fiber of her being was grafting onto his, and she let it.

The sweet interlude was over too fast. Grant backed away first. "I want to keep kissing you, but we shouldn't. I don't think either of us is ready for that." Lightning flashed and lit the room in bright white, and the thunder clapped again. He took her in his arms until the shaking was done. "It looks like you're staying the night, though. Can we just talk?"

Thandie was not offended in the slightest. He wanted boundaries, and so did she. "I'd like that."

CHAPTER 21

Grant looked at the sleeping beauty on the floor in front of the smoldering cinders in the fireplace. Thandie had slept peacefully for hours now. He didn't know what time they had finally dozed off, though sleep didn't permit him much rest. Waking in a panic at the raging storm outside sometime in the black of night, he had paced the modest room and checked for more roof leaks. Finding no new drips, he emptied the nearly overflowing bowl of rainwater and placed it back on the floor.

With a chill in the air, he stoked what remained of the fire, knowing that all the rest of the wood was likely soaked outside. Grant covered Thandie with another blanket where she lay on the fur rug by the heat. Her skin radiated a warm glow, and her face was relaxed and smooth. He stayed awake and made certain that she rested unburdened by the events happening outdoors.

From a comfortable place in the crook of the leather chair's back and armrest, he lounged until the first light of day brightened the windows. The rain still pounded the roof, although the thunder had stopped sometime in the night. In the dim light outside, he saw the damage left by the storm, likely to worsen if the rains continued.

The path leading to the barn was now a river. Tree limbs, full of new spring growth, were scattered across the lawn, and one whole tree had crashed over the split rail fence that led down to the dock. Out the front window, the once dry lakebed looked like a growing pond. Grant gazed out over the waters and could imagine what this place would have looked like in its summertime prime.

He could see Thandie leading a group of guests across the water in small canoes or teetering atop paddleboards, the sun highlighting the brighter bits of her hair and causing her already tan skin to darken. He'd come back for a retreat like *that* if The Foundry survived until then.

Outside, a bell rang out from the direction of the barn, loud and sharp enough to cut through the rain hitting the roof, and robbed him of his contemplation.

Thandie sat up and rubbed her eyes. "What is that?" she said as she got her bearings.

"Sounds like it's coming from the barn," Grant said. "Good morning."

The bell continued with no letup.

"Oh gosh." Thandie took stock of the surroundings.

Her eyes went to the empty bottle of wine, the skewers resting at the threshold of the fire, and her robe that had opened slightly but didn't expose anything. She promptly and discreetly crossed the front sides of the robe and held it tight at her neck. He sensed her unease, perhaps embarrassment or vulnerability, in waking up on some man's floor. Giving her space, he stayed back near the front windows.

"It's bad out there," he said. "Why don't you get dressed and I'll call up to the barn and see what's going on."

"I don't have anything to wear. My things are all in my cabin." She gestured to her robe as though he didn't see that she was only wearing the white fluffy garment, which he most definitely was aware of.

"I did the laundry. The power came back on, and I threw your things in from yesterday," he said with pride evident in his tone.

"You cleaned my clothes?" she said and looked like she wanted to die. Her hands covered her face.

"Did I do something wrong?" He didn't think he had. He was very respectful and neat in the manner in which he did their laundry. "I was awake, and I knew you would want something more than that to wear today. Nor would you want to be seen leaving my cabin in only a bathrobe."

She looked down at her garment and nodded. "I appreciate it, I do. Thank you." She pointed to the bathroom and raised an eyebrow.

"It's all folded on the counter in there."

Thandie stood and walked to the bathroom door. "This place has a laundry?"

"There's a machine in the kitchen, under the cabinet beside the sink. It's small, but it does both the wash and the dry," Grant said and walked to her. "I thought I was doing the right thing, but I apologize if I've offended you."

"You haven't." Thandie brushed some of her curls back from her face. Her color was high on her cheeks. She craned onto her toes and planted a kiss on his cheek. "Thank you. It was kind of you to wash my panties. No man has ever done my laundry before, is all."

The door closed in front of him, and he stood in stunned silence. The way she said panties was the sexiest thing he'd ever heard. A deep breath and a headshake later, he made himself busy cleaning up the night's mess. He started by washing the dishes, folding blankets, fluffing pillows, and doing anything else to take his mind off of her getting dressed in those pink lace panties that he had so expertly laid out for her.

Grant was already dressed and ready for the day, though he hadn't predicted the morning beginning with church bells. He picked up the phone and dialed the office extension. Even after several rings, no one picked up. With the rain still pouring outside, he wasn't prepared to go out in it just yet, and the only window in the cabin that viewed the barn was in the bathroom. "Thandie, can you see the barn from in there?" he said through the door.

"Um . . ." she said, and it sounded as though she stumbled over something and caught herself on the porcelain sink. She giggled. "I'm okay, but I can't see the barn well. The rain is too heavy. Did you get anyone on the phone?"

"No one answered. We should head that way, right?" he said.

Thandie opened the bathroom door and was finishing tucking in her blue shirt at the waist of her black cargo shorts. Folding her clothes in the middle of the night, he had only noticed her delicate pink undergarments. And on the nature walk, he had been too preoccupied with his darn gesture to see what she was wearing. He had hoped the flowers would make her day, but instead, they messed him up. What was worse was the way he had reacted to the fear grappling inside of him.

She pulled her hair back into a low ponytail and slicked back the sides where her hair was curlier. "I used your hair paste. I hope that's alright."

Of course it was okay. He had done a good job showing her what kind of person he was and that he wouldn't be offended by her use of his products. She was comfortable with him, and that was exactly where he hoped she would be. The alternative was that she was a thief, albeit an honest one. He nodded and took in the sight of her.

She was stunning, and natural. And worried.

Her brows pinched together in the middle, and although she tried for a smile, her mouth turned down at the corners. Without her asking, he embraced her and wrapped his arms around her shoulders. She leaned into him, and her body relaxed into his as though they were meant to fit together. The moment was carefree, until the bells rang out again, tensing her muscles beneath his hands.

"I'd offer you coffee, but I don't think we have time for that. How 'bout a jacket instead?"

"I appreciate it, but you should stay here out of the weather," she suggested.

"Like hell I will. I'm not letting you go up there alone." He handed her his flannel jacket and a poncho with The Foundry logo printed on the back. She slipped both items on and tied her boot laces—pink, he noted—while he retrieved a slick yellow raincoat from the little closet outside the bathroom. "You ready?"

She nodded, and he opened the door to a blast of cold, damp air. The mist hit his face, and he recoiled from the shock to his skin. He took her hand, and they dashed into the rain towards the barn. Between dodging downed limbs and puddles, the ground squished beneath his feet as they ran across the field. It was the most direct route and the only way not washed out between his place and the barn.

As they got close, the door opened. Margret's head poked out and she waved them inside. Thandie went first and Grant helped close the door upon making it through. The bells rang out from nearby again, and he looked around for the source of the sound.

"What's with the bells?" Grant asked Margret as he caught Anne's eyes where she sat in the *cucina*. "Have you both been in here all night?"

"Afraid so," Anne said. Her face drooped from lack of sleep, and he realized his mug unlikely looked any better.

"We were in here waiting for dinner when the storm hit hard. Been here since," Margret said. "As for the bells, Leo has been out there ringing them for a while. The telephone lines are down, and he mentioned Pa would know what to do."

"I know Pa," Thandie said and shook the water off her poncho. Her eyes trained on the scene outside the glass doors.

"What do you see, dear?" Margret asked.

"It looks like some of the other guests are heading this way too. I wonder if there's flooding in any of their cabins, or perhaps they heard the bells like we did and are coming to see what's going on."

Grant helped push the door open against the wind and let the two younger couples indoors. "Did you have any flooding at your cabins?" he asked.

"No, but it's a swamp," Brent said.

The woman on his arm added, "The lake is filling back up. All those pretty flowers—gone!" she turned to Thandie. "I'm so glad we went on the nature walk while we still could. It was so beautiful."

Thandie took her hands. "It'll all come back. It's only water."

"What if the lake stays filled?" Grant asked her as though she was a water expert.

She shrugged. "I guess we go for a swim." That made everyone laugh, though nervously. "Look. He's here."

Grant flipped his raincoat hood up and walked out to meet the older gentleman. Driving his old blue pickup truck, Pa towed a flatbed piled high with sand. Coming to a stop right in front of the building, Pa hopped out, and Grant shook the old man's hand. "Pa? Hi, I'm Grant. How can we help?"

Pa motioned for Grant to follow him around to the bed of the truck. He dropped the tailgate, where hundreds of sandbags were bundled and stacked. "We need these filled up. The bridge washed out, and all that water is coming this way if the rain doesn't let up soon."

Grant pointed at the lake. "It's already here."

"We better move fast," Pa said with an uneasy chuckle. He pointed to the side of the barn. "Shovels are back there."

Grant returned to the flatbed with the tools. Thandie stood beside the sand pile, unpacking the bags. Even Brent and the other man, William, came out of the barn to lend a hand. They all got straight to work. Everyone knew what needed to be done.

Thandie and Pa held the bags open. Grant and Brent shoveled loads into the bags. William tied them off and passed the filled sandbag to Leo. The bags were passed down the line of volunteers that wrapped around to the back of the barn where he could only assume some flooding or erosion was in progress. Grant didn't realize when so many people had shown up to help, but he recognized them all as the other guests. Even the trio of older ladies was out there in their galoshes, swinging sand.

The once-dry creek that bordered the property swelled to the brim. What looked like a landscape feature running along the long path from the barn down to the old dock was now a torrent, threatening the stunning barn itself. The sandbags were their only hope now. Even if by some miracle they got the job done today, he knew that waterways often overflowed their banks after the storm was long gone. Getting the investment was the least of The Foundry's worries, now surviving the day was on the line.

In no time, they used up all the sandbags in creating a barrier about two feet high along the back of the barn where the stream turned before making the last straight run into the lake. Grant hoped it would be enough. He had become very fond of the retreat and was willing to do whatever he could to save it.

"Thanks for the help," Pa said and climbed into the driver's seat. "I'm going for another load."

Thandie led everyone back inside the barn to get warm and dry until Pa returned. Leo was the last one in, and instead of stopping and taking a break, he ran toward the back of the barn nearest to where the stream came closest to the structure. Seeing dread on Leo's face, Grant took Thandie's hand, and they followed behind Leo.

How could the man not be worried? After all, everything Leo had worked for, all the time and preparation to get the retreat up and going, looked like it was at risk of washing away in an instant. His heart went out to the man who had been nothing but a gracious host the whole week thus far.

Thandie flexed her fingers around Grant's as their feet sloshed through a half inch of water. Grant's suspicions were confirmed in the exercise area. The rubber carpets were soaked, and rain spilled in from the window ledge like a waterfall. The flooding wasn't coming from the rising waters at all, but from a poorly sealed window. A window that could be fixed if they acted quick enough.

"What can we do?" Thandie asked and let go of Grant's hand.

"I can't afford to replace all this stuff," Leo said. "Will you bring as much as you can carry up to the loft or in the *cucina*?"

"Grant, I could use your help outside with a tarp."

"Let's go," Grant said, and the two men ran back through the barn.

Grant didn't see Thandie again for a while, as their routes were opposite. From outside the window, he could tell that she was working hard as the various equipment stocks inside dwindled. Leo met him with a hammer and nails, a tarp, and a scrap board. Pinning the tarp behind the board, Grant held it all in place while Leo hammered in the nails. It was an ugly fix, but it would keep the majority of the driving rain off of the failing window until a permanent fix could be made.

On his way back in, Pa pulled around and parked by the door with an empty flatbed.

"Pa, what happened?" Leo asked, but Pa was out of breath. "Why don't you come inside really quick."

Leo escorted the older man, and Grant held the door, snapping his fingers for someone to bring a chair over to them. Inside, Pa plopped into the seat without a complaint, and someone else handed him a water bottle.

"The road . . . is . . . gone," he said between sips.

"Which road," Leo asked, "the one out of town?"

"County Line is completely washed out. We've got to get these people out of here before the last one goes, too," Pa said.

"Are you alright?" Grant asked and crouched down to the old man's eye level.

"Nearly took me out, it did. I threw the truck in reverse as soon as I saw the banks crumble into the water, but the gravel just rolled under the weight of the trailer. It's a miracle that the tires finally caught some traction when they did, or I would have been lost in the drink."

"Goodness," Thandie said. "I'm glad you're okay."

"So, we need to evacuate?" Anne chimed in.

"City Hall," Leo said. "It sits on the highest point around here. We can wait out the storm there and then get you all to the train station in Elizabethtown later today or tomorrow," Leo said with shakiness in his voice. "I'm so sorry that this has happened during your stay—"

"You didn't make it rain," Grant said, repeating what he had told Thandie last night. "You have nothing to be sorry for. I can speak for me, and probably everyone else here that we have had an amazing time at The Foundry."

Other voices joined him in agreement. It was seemingly unanimous that they had all had a fulfilling stay there.

Tears welled in Leo's eyes. "Thank you all. I want to offer you each a complimentary stay here in the future, if we come out of this okay." He wiped his cheek. "Now, can you each be packed and back here in twenty minutes? We'll depart as soon as possible."

The others darted outside into the rain to gather their things. Leo looked at Thandie, and she simply shook her head back at him as though to say she was not going. She moved toward Grant with determination in her serious face. "You need to get your things. It's not safe to stay here," she said and poked a finger into his sternum.

He captured her little finger and held her hand flat on his chest. "I'm not going anywhere."

"Grant, you have to. It's a liability thing, since you're a guest here."

"Then I'll check out." He raised his voice. "Hey Leo, I'm checking out, you cool with that?"

"If you want to stay, then stay," Leo said from across the *cucina*, where he was stacking chairs on top of the tables.

"Looks like I'm staying right here. With you." He intended his voice to sound loving and protective, but there was a slight hesitation in his own words, at the implications of his statement. Though he was sure he was ready to move forward with his life, he wasn't sure she was, or that she was feeling what he was feeling. It was awfully presumptuous of him, and with a little more time together, he hoped she would open up to him more.

"If you're staying, then get to work." She pointed at the *cucina*. "Why don't you see if anything needs to be moved in there? And make us some sandwiches while you're at it."

"I'm on it." Grant said again at yet another task he was more than happy to do.

Pa stood near the *cucina* door as Grant began toward that direction. "You know, I'm usually the one taking orders around here. It's nice to see someone else being told what to do for a change."

Grant chuckled, knowing there was more to that story that he would want to hear about some day. Just the thought of wanting to get to know more about the people around him was another indication that he was changing, moving on, for the better. "I'm happy to help."

"This place is something special. It means a lot to the community, and I know we are all glad you're pitching in here today." Pa took Grant's hand in his firm grip and shook it in gratitude.

"Take care making it to the city hall." They exchanged a nod of understanding, and Pa was off.

As ordered, Grant went through the *cucina* doors and got to work on those sandwiches.

CHAPTER 22

Later, after the work was done enough, Thandie stood in the heat of the shower. Though she was saturated and sick of being wet, the hot water running over her cold skin soothed her weary muscles. Her hair, that she never liked all that much for the fact that it was only curly enough to always be tangled, needed a second run through of her conditioner. As she worked the cream into her ends, she inhaled long deep breaths into her lungs, preferring the warm lavender scented air to the musky damp odor of the mud outside.

Just beyond the door to her bathroom, a man whom she was accidentally falling for waited for her to finish up. Before sheltering in her cabin for the night, he had run to his room and packed up all of his things. It made no sense for him to stay and deal with the leaky roof, although he did say he had put a larger bucket under the leak in hopes of saving what he could of the place. A thoughtful gesture.

They had worked all day at securing the barn from the rising and falling waters. Pa had delivered the guests to safety, and Leo had joined them in town, where he planned to stay at America's house on Main Street. He assured Thandie that he would be safe there, and that if anything changed, he would send Pa to come back for her and Grant. There was nothing left for them to do but wait it out.

During the day, the power had stayed on, despite the rain ebbing long enough to get their hopes up, then returning with harder downpours. She hadn't seen anything like it before in the Midwest where, if it rained at all, the storms would come on fast and leave even faster. The forecast she had looked up at the start of the week proved to be dead wrong.

With the last of the conditioner rinsed out, Thandie turned the shower off and reached for a towel hanging on a hook just outside the white shower curtain. Drying off took no time at all as she didn't wish to be wet any longer than was absolutely necessary. In this instance, she wanted nothing more than to put on her coziest pants and socks, wrap up in a fluffy blanket and sip wine by the fire.

Her wish was granted when she emerged from the bathroom, dressed in lightweight cotton pants and a matching pale pink henley tank top, to a scene straight out of a romance novel. As she walked out, using a hand towel to scrunch the water from her hair and give some life to her curls, Grant stood in front of the fire. His hand rested casually on the mantel, and he fixed his eyes on the glass of an old clock ticking the time by.

She threw her hair towel over the back of a stool and cleared her throat. "Ahem."

He turned, a lowball filled with an amber liquid in his hand, and smirked. He was devastatingly handsome, with stubble shadowing his cheekbones and jawline. *That man should need a license for being single and looking the way he looks with his buttery skin and tousled, wavy hair*, she thought.

She bit her lip and blinked slowly to make certain he was real. "Shower's yours," she said.

He met her in the middle of the space and handed her his glass.

There was a marked lack of words between them. Perhaps they were too exhausted to talk, or perhaps there was so much to say and neither of them wanted to start that conversation. She sipped his whisky and watched him take his suitcase into the bathroom. He closed the door, and she heard the shower start, her cue to take a load off for a few minutes. She let the couch absorb her, and she sank deep into the pillows while allowing her eyes to close.

Grant Goldie, she said in her mind. *Thandie Goldie? No, that's bad. Thandeka Goldie is better.*

An image played out in her mind. She was walking down the small aisle of a rural church, bathed in the sunlight that was streaming through stained glass windows and painting the room in warm colors. She knew the exercise was futile, but it meant she was ready to move on all the same. And why not with Grant Goldie?

When she opened her eyes, she was no longer on the couch. It was no longer dark outside. Sunshine streamed in through the windows in her room and illuminated tiny dust particles floating through the air. Tucked beneath the fluffy down comforter and crisp sheets, she was alone in her bed. She sat up and searched for Grant. Last she knew, he was showering.

He must have put her to bed sometime after she dozed, relaxing on the couch, though she had no recollection of him moving her, let alone him coming out of the bathroom. The previous day had caught up to her and knocked her out. Nothing could have kept her from sleep last night, not even her thumping heart or the butterflies fluttering in her belly at the sight of Grant's roguish smirk.

She tiptoed to the living room and saw her knight in shining armor lying peacefully on the sofa in front of the fireplace, its faux embers still glowing between the black-and-gray logs. An empty glass lay tipped on its side on the floor below him, where his hand hung off the side of the couch. A pillow propped up his head on the armrest, and a blanket hung halfway off of him, exposing his shirtless top half.

She righted the glass and kneeled down beside him. His face was calm and his skin smooth. He had shaved the stubble from his cheeks, and a tiny piece of toilet tissue stuck to his chin where he had likely nicked himself. Thandie liked the stubble, but his clean skin begged to be touched.

Taking his hand that hung off the side of the cushions, she laid it across his upper body. She traced the outline where his ribs met his abs and continued upward to his well-formed chest muscles.

He cracked an eye open. It was only a sliver, but she knew she was caught. "Good morning," she said and pulled the blanket up over his chest as if that's what she was doing all along. He responded with that dangerous grin again, the one that pulled at one cheek and lit a fire in his eyes. The one that she looked forward to seeing, to reacting to.

"Morning," he said. "Did you sleep well?"

She nodded. "Thank you for putting me to bed last night."

"Of course. You needed a good night's sleep after the week you've had. Do you feel any better this morning?"

"I do," she said, and the words felt thick with meaning. She shook her head and stood away from his heat. "Coffee?"

Thandie didn't wait for an answer. She needed coffee, and she would make some coffee.

Grant stood, and the blanket fell off his bare chest. He threw it over the couch's armrest and stretched his arms high over his head. "How about I get dressed while you do that?"

She nodded and stared, though she tried not to, at his sculpted body, his booty-hugging, light gray sweatpants—Grant tugged at the cotton rope strings at his waist which brought more attention to the area—his white crew socks, and his wavy hair falling down by his left eye. "Yes. Definitely go put some clothes on."

He chuckled in his throat and moved towards the bathroom. He passed through a beam of light, spilling in through the east-facing window, and illuminated his skin like marble. Looking away for fear of losing herself, she wiped her forehead with the kitchen towel and shook the swooning away. The bathroom door closed, and her hand flew to her forehead.

"What are you doing Thandeka Nkosi?" Thandie scolded herself while the coffeepot began percolating. Moving around the space, she picked up the dishes and straightened the couch cushions. Pulling back the curtains from the south-facing window, the previous day's turmoil was evident. The place was wrecked. Downed trees, a seemingly new river running through the property, washed out sections of the pathways, and wooden roof shingles were scattered all over. This was not good.

Saturday was meant to be the guests' final morning and checkout. She had planned a trust course followed by a luncheon barbeque, but now there would be none of that. The guests had all checked out and been evacuated to the town yesterday evening, and for all she knew, would not be coming back anytime soon.

The pot beeped. "Milk?" she yelled, so that Grant could hear through the wooden bathroom door, as she splashed some into her own cup.

"Black," he said, though his voice was muffled. Before she finished pouring his coffee, he emerged from the bathroom wearing his signature khaki cargo pants, white t-shirt, and plaid button-down. A smile plastered from ear to ear as though not smiling would be more painful. She knew this smile well.

"Do you own any other clothes?" she teased.

"Well," he said and showed off his outfit. "I thought this would be appropriate for today. Cool, casual, but still pulled together, attractive, but not memorable. And"—he took a long sip of his drink—"you like my plaid shirts."

He got the attractive part right, and it would be a difficult task to ever forget about Grant Goldie. Thinking of her own repeated outfit, at least he had had the chance to pack. She only had the clothing that she had thrown into her suitcase in haste when she had left her home a few months earlier, and no spare money to buy anything more than was essential. Her cute activewear was better suited for gym photoshoots than it was for hiking in the rain, but she had made it work.

Judging by how the week had gone, Thandie guessed she would be on the job hunt again. There was no way that the investor would give the money The Foundry needs now. No matter how much attention she showed the guests, how delicious the food was, or how wonderful the accommodations were, there was no way to overcome the obvious drawbacks of a retreat that featured more rain than anything else.

Though she was unsure whether Grant was the person sent by the investor, she still wanted to know his thoughts. "As the activities director here at The Foundry, can I ask you a question?" He nodded while taking another sip of his coffee. "If you could ignore all the rain, how would you rate your experience here?"

His eyes darted to the rafters, and he took a long moment before answering. "Nine out of ten."

"Really? Nine?" His rating was suspicious in that she didn't believe it. "How do you figure?"

Grant came around and stood in front of her. He put his mug down on the counter, and exchanged the coffee cup in her grasp for his hands. He looked at her with such purity of intentions that she shifted away, uncomfortable at the intimacy between them.

"What?" she said and tried looking away, but he caught her gaze no matter where she looked.

He nudged her chin up to face him. "Coming here and meeting you has been a gift."

"A gift?"

"Yes. I need to say something here." Grant hushed her. "I was hurting. For years. I know you didn't ask the other night, even though you wanted to know. I appreciate you giving me some time to wrap my mind around telling you or not." He paused and closed his eyes as though he was looking at prepared remarks behind his lids. "I'm a widower."

Silence hung between them as she considered what to say to his admission. "Oh, Grant, I'm so sorry." Thandie was not expecting that word to come out of his mouth. *Widower.* She had a dozen questions. "How did she—" Thandie stopped herself. Grant had asked her to let him finish.

"It's okay. I want to tell you. I need to tell you. I married an incredible woman right after high school. We were young and in love, and she was gone too soon." He swallowed hard, and his Adam's apple bobbed down and back up before he continued. "My wife passed away nearly ten years ago. It was sudden. She had an allergic reaction to a medication. I called for help, but it was too late by the time the ambulance arrived."

Thandie remained silent, but her mind targeted one thing alone. The way he overreacted to the skin rash caused by the flowers must have triggered the gut-wrenching memory. He had experienced a panic attack almost immediately. It was no wonder that he had. Now that she had the information—the tragic information at that—she understood.

"Thandie," he gripped her hands tightly, "The agony of her loss was more than I could suffer. I've been running from it, from everything, so that I wouldn't feel anything. And then—and then I ran right into you. And you, along with this place, have given me the freedom to feel again in ways I didn't think I was capable of any longer." He bit back a whimper and blinked the tears away. "I don't know what, if anything, I can promise you, but if nothing else comes from this experience, I am forever grateful to have spent this week here at The Foundry—here with you."

"I don't know what to say." And she didn't. Tears rolled down her cheeks as fear gripped her throat at what he would proclaim to her next.

With the back of his hand, Grant stroked the tears away with a tenderness she hadn't seen from him before. "If this is our last day together . . ." Grant paused and lifted her up. He sat her bottom on the edge of the cold countertop and nestled his hips between her thighs. "I would like to kiss you again before we leave this cabin, and before the world catches up to us. Right now. In this minute." Grant brushed a stray curl behind her ear and rested his hand on the back of her neck as he awaited her answer.

There were no words.

She draped her arms around his shoulders. Her eyes answered with a long blink. She wanted nothing more than to kiss him again and feel his soft, warm lips caress hers with tenderness and passion. He leaned in and they were joined together. Two adults who were healing their past hurt, not for each other, but alongside one another.

The kiss was different than the previous one. Longer. Deeper. His lips hugged hers in an embrace and had a healing property of their own. She knew from the way his hand trailed down her spine to her lower back, and the tilt of his head that gave them the perfect closeness, and the small flutter in his breathing, that their union, no matter how long, was the sort of remedy they both needed.

Wedding bells played in her mind with her eyes closed and her lips and body pressed against Grant. Her hands explored the curves of his chest and back while he held her snug against him. A flash of a future with him appeared in her mind. A vision where she walked through the cornfields of Iowa hand in hand with this most unexpected stranger.

CHAPTER 23

Without warning, the stranger in her daydream pulled away from her and nudged her back into reality. As she opened her eyes, she realized the wedding bells weren't ringing in her mind at all but were coming from the direction of the barn. "Do you hear that?" she asked, to make sure she wasn't hallucinating, while her heart danced in her chest from the best kiss she had ever enjoyed.

"It's probably Leo, like yesterday. We should head that way and see what's up." Grant took his mug and downed the rest of his coffee, winking at her over the rim.

They threw on their shoes and jackets and headed the short distance to the barn. The damage was worse the closer they got. The stream, usually dry, was a torrent as it ripped around the back side of the barn, though the structure looked to be intact. Leo emerged from the side of the barn with three shovels and work gloves.

"You ready to get to work?" Leo asked and handed the gloves to Thandie. He turned his attention to Grant and shook his hand. "You know, I appreciate you staying with her last night. And please feel free to head out of town whenever you need to."

Grant took gloves and a shovel. "If it's all right with you, I'd like to stay." He grinned at Thandie. "So, Activities Director Thandie, what is on the schedule for today?"

She giggled at how professional he sounded. "I think we're going to do some earth moving, followed by water remediation. Sound good?"

"Sounds like a plan to me."

The three of them made their way around the barn and assessed the damage. The ground had held through the night where the stream turned a corner and all the sandbags had stayed securely in place. They got to work cutting a shallow ditch around the other side of the barn and down toward the dock. Other than the dirt being heavy and swollen from all the rain, it dug out easily. By mid-morning, the ditch was just about complete.

Leo and Grant ran back up and dug out the remaining few inches. Water began traveling down their new trench and relieved the pressure from the stream. They watched as the new trench filled to the brim and poured into the lake.

"Will you look at that?" Leo said. "Just like it used to be."

"But how? There's no dam holding the water back," Thandie said.

"Christmas Cove was always a deeper section of the lake. I suppose it'll hold some, for now anyway," Leo said with a hopeful but realistic tone in his voice. The tone of a man that really wanted to be optimistic but had been let down before.

As they viewed their hard work, behind them, vehicles crested the road, honking their horns. A convoy of pickup trucks, heavy bulldozers, and backhoes came down the road and stopped in front of the barn.

Pa led the way from the cab of his blue pickup. Parking beside Leo's red truck in the drive, he climbed out and rubbed his hands together. "I brought help." Pa turned and helped out an older woman with silvery white hair pinned into a knot at the top of her head. America hopped down from the passenger side door and waved them over.

"What is all this?" Leo asked and gave America a quick kiss on the cheek. "How did you get here? I thought the big bridge washed out."

"It held. And thank goodness it did, or we wouldn't be here to help you, but I see you got a start without us." Pa pointed over his shoulder at the man driving the bulldozer. "Look who came to help. Be nice."

"Will you look at that?" Leo said and shook his head.

"That's right. Your brother, the mayor, called this morning and asked how the city could help. And here he is with the full power of Elizabethtown."

Leo's eyes were wide, and his brows raised like mountains on his forehead.

"What am I missing?" Grant asked.

The older woman pushed the men aside and bobbled her head back and forth as she spoke. "Hi, I'm Carol. I live in town, and I know everything about everything. So, here's the short of it. Leo here used to be the mayor of Christmas Cove, and his brother, John, is the mayor of neighboring Elizabethtown. Let's just say they aren't exactly best friends, so when Christmas Cove was incorporated by Elizabethtown, Leo lost his job, and his brother won." She looked at Leo. "Does that about cover it?"

"Just about," Leo said without taking his gaze off of his brother.

"You should be glad," Pa whispered, leaning into Leo's side. "This is the first real test of the new city agreement. And here they are, doing what needs to be done."

"I suppose I should go give my thanks, then."

"And marching orders," Pa added.

As Leo got everyone squared away with assignments, the big equipment got to work. A dump truck emptied new, crushed gravel for the road and driveway. Another digger cleaned up and widened the hand-dug trench. A crew of townsfolk walked the grounds and picked up debris and trash.

Above them, the sun shone bright and hot, and the air was thick with humidity and hope. Before long, more people arrived. The Foundry was teeming with helpers. Chainsaws whined and made easy work of the fallen trees. Some people fixed roofs, while others ripped out soaking drywall from inside some of the cabins that hadn't fared as well as hers. The carpets were cleaned and bedding stripped.

Thandie helped where she could, and the day passed by quickly. The chef had put out a spread of food on buffet tables just inside the propped open barn doors, and Thandie was determined now, more than ever, to track him down and make a proper introduction. Starving, and ready to eat a whole cow, she made her way to the dumpster with a final load of debris piled high in the bike cart before marching into the barn.

Just outside the barn doors, Leo talked with America, who was holding a plate of food. Seeing the food only made Thandie's mouth water more. She walked by them, not wanting to be sidetracked by their serious-looking conversation.

Passing the food, she flew through the saloon-style *cucina* doors, which bounced off the door frame and nearly took her out when they rebounded. "Hello?" she sang into the sterile room. "Chef? Are you in here?"

From the open walk-in refrigerator, sounds of plastic food bins scraping and hitting against each other were followed by grunts, and what sounded like cursing echoed against the stainless-steel surfaces.

"Chef?" Thandie said and came around the corner. "Chef?"

He turned, startled, and removed his earbuds. "Out. Go out of my *cucina*," he said in a cute Italian accent while shooing her back towards the door with exaggerated sweeps of his arms.

"Wait. Chef. Stop," she said and pushed back against his shoulders. "I'm Thandie. I work here." She waited for her words to sink in, and a sheepish grin pulled his cheek up on one side. "I wanted to thank you."

"Yes, of course, Thandeka. Celiac like Alfonso, no?" Alfonso reached out and took her hand between both of his, shaking them up and down in a wild manner.

Through a giggle, Thandie said, "It's nice to finally meet you."

"And me to you." Letting go of her hand, he turned and walked back to the walk-in. "This is all bad. All of it."

"The food?" she said and peeked inside, where he was throwing items into surplus cardboard boxes. "When the power went out?"

"I do not know. I dislike very much this, how you say? Tossing out?"

"Yes, I think that is the right word. Let me help you. I'm sure it's not as bad as you think." They sorted the last couple of crates on the floor, and Thandie used the moment to get to know him a bit. There was one question that she was eager to know the answer to. "Can I ask you about supper on the first night? It seemed you made dishes from the guests' preference sheets—"

"Yes. I did. What is the question?"

"Did you intend on making the foods that people indicated that they don't like?"

"Do not like? How you know what you like and what you do not like until you try Alfonso cooking?"

Thandie considered the chef's words. How does one know for certain about anything? Sometimes you just have to see things from a new perspective. That sentiment is easier said than done in reality. She acknowledged Alfonso with an affirmative grunt.

"Supper was wonderful. And thank you for your hard work this week," she said. "I think we're all finished here, and my tummy is growling for some of that delicious food that you put out."

He stood up and brushed his hands on his blue apron. "*Grazi.*" He pointed to the tidied mess.

"You're welcome," she said and went straight to the buffet.

Out by the doors, she was indiscriminate in her selection. Everything looked appetizing. She took a whole-grain wrap and layered a piece of fresh-cut turkey with lettuce, tomato, and a slice of cheddar cheese. On another table, Alfonso had put out platters of fresh-cut fruit and veggies and a basket filled with individual bags of potato chips. She took one of everything.

Preferring to sit outside, Thandie turned to the doors where the late afternoon sunlight shone in and blinded her. She saw the silhouette of a person passing through, and they crashed shoulder to shoulder. Her plate of food slid from her hands, but the quick reactions of the other person saved it and replaced it in her grasp.

"I'm so sorry," she said. "I couldn't see very well with the sun shining this way."

"It was my fault. I was looking the other way and didn't see anyone at all." The man helped stabilize her.

She pulled down her sunglasses from the top of her head. Her eyes always watered in bright sunlight, and she blinked the wetness away, though she was certain she was hallucinating when the man came into clear view. "Davis?"

"Surprise!" he said with a joker of a smile.

"What are you doing here?"

"Grant told me you were here," Davis said and pulled her to the side and out of the doorway so that one of the city workers could pass.

"Grant told you?" Just how Davis and Grant knew each other well enough to be speaking about her in any capacity was a question she desperately wanted an answer to. Was he spying on her somehow?

"What are you doing all the way out here, anyway?" Davis said as if nothing was strange about this encounter.

"I work here."

He began to giggle and cleared his throat. "This place needs a botanist?"

"I'm the activities director. And you don't need to laugh," she said, putting down her plate on a little table, having lost her appetite. The man had never laughed at anything out of genuine joy, and now he finds something amusing about her situation, a situation he drove her to.

"So, you're some kind of camp counselor?"

She could tell he was holding in a laugh again. When Grant had teased her with the same title, she wasn't in the least offended, but when Davis said it, she was reminded in no uncertain terms that she had dodged a bullet when he had walked out on her the night before their wedding.

"I shouldn't have said it that way." Davis shrugged, but Thandie recognized that his words still fell short of an actual apology. "I found out from your cousin that you were heading this way. Only he didn't know exactly which retreat you were working at in the area. You know that I've been looking at investing on the East Coast for a while now—"

"You have?"

"Of course, silly. So, when I found out that you had a new job around here, I put out some feelers."

"So, what you mean to say is that you were spying on me?"

"What? No." Davis was quick to answer. "Technically, I had no idea that you worked here, at this specific location. But I hoped to find you at one of the resorts and have that reunion. I care about you, isn't that clear—"

"You care about something, that's for sure, but I don't know if it's me," Thandie said, and it felt good to speak her truth for once. "What do you want, Davis?" Not that it mattered anymore. He didn't matter to her anymore. She had let go of the hurt and self-doubt of the past and was ready, for the first time in months, to see a new future for herself. A future that did not include ex-fiancés. "Did that slut from Vegas dump you or something?"

He shook his head back and forth with a grimace.

"She did, didn't she?" Too much satisfaction licked at Thandie's words. "How did it feel?"

"Awful," Davis said. "And I told you that I made a mistake. I meant it."

Thandie recognized that Davis claiming he made a mistake was not the same as an apology, but wondered if he was too proud to say it. "Is this about your voicemail?" she asked.

"Oh, so you did get it. Good!" he chuckled for no reason at all, which chafed her again.

She crossed her arms in front of her chest, the way she did whenever she was on defense. "Why are you here, Davis?"

"For you. Is that so hard to believe?"

"Yes," she said. "I didn't know you were the potential investor here, or I would have—"

"Invited me sooner?" he finished. "I wish you would have. This place is a disaster. Not what I thought I'd be walking into today, to be honest," he added and seemed to be looking past her and out to the property. "Grant's my consultant, and he made this place out to be a paradise."

"He did?" Thandie said, and her heart filled with gladness at such a glowing report about the week, despite the terrible weather.

"You know Grant. He's great, right? Professional and to the point."

Thandie kicked the ground on the way out into the sun. "How could I be so stupid?" He'd been the spy all along and she didn't notice? Or she did suspect and wouldn't admit the glaring truth to herself. She had convinced herself that the consultant was the bubbly Daisy and her disinterested Brent, and had ruled Grant out. Like an idiot.

Davis followed her outside. "Are you alright? You seem agitated," he said.

She took a breath and relaxed into a pleasant face devoid of the ire she felt pressurizing in her chest. "Everything is fine."

Davis reached for her hand and held it the way he used to with his fingers intertwined with hers. What used to be a comfort now felt wrong, and she pulled her hand back and faced him.

"I know that when you say you're fine, you're not. But no matter. I'm here now, and I have some business to get to. We can have a proper reunion later." Davis leaned in and pressed his lips to hers. Holding her shoulders awkwardly, she was stiff as a cornstalk in October under his touch.

"Thandie?" Grant's voice sounded from behind her.

Suddenly wanting to die, she rolled her eyes towards the sky, hoping to see a guardian angel there to save her from the blowback she was certain was about to hit. "Hi, Grant. I didn't know you were standing there."

"I see that," Grant said with a shake in his voice. The same shake that had been present when he had spilled his heart to her about losing his wife so tragically.

She took a step toward him, and he took an equal step away from her. "Grant . . ." she reached for him, but he didn't reach back. Instead, Davis caught her hand in midair and held her fingers intertwined with his.

"This Davis, is *your* Davis?" Grant asked.

Davis tugged on her arm so that she faced him again. "You told him that I was *your* Davis? So, you did get that voicemail. I was wondering because I never heard back from you, and I meant every single word. I want you back Than. I made the biggest mistake of my life letting you go." Davis pulled her closer and locked her in an embrace. His lips crushed against hers and she was helpless to get away. His moan at their sudden connection turned her stomach.

Thandie slid her hands between them up to his chest and used her own body as leverage to push him away, but it was too late. When she finally freed herself from Davis's hold, Grant was gone.

CHAPTER 24

"So, is that a yes?" Davis asked.

"You cannot be serious. Do you really want to do this right now?" Thandie walked back inside, half looking for Grant, and half looking for some food to fill her mouth with. Chewing a sandwich was preferable to chewing him out in front of everyone. She wanted to say all the things that she had stored up for months, but it wasn't the time nor the place for such an eruption. "Look around. Can't you see there are more important things that need to be done right now than this?" She gestured back and forth between them.

"Like taking a bulldozer to this place?" He laughed without humor.

"That's incredibly insensitive, Davis," she scolded him. "You have no idea what these people—what I went through in the last twenty-four hours. Grant told you this was a paradise, and until yesterday, it was." She found her plate of food and walked back outside.

America met her near the door and whispered. "That man you're talking to is the investor."

Thandie knew exactly who he was, and she was quite aware

that she held a metaphorical wrench that could put the entire deal in jeopardy. She nodded and chewed a little slower as she let the events play out. America escorted her back inside to the *cucina*, where Leo and Davis shook hands. Thandie stayed quiet and continued stuffing her cheeks.

"Oh good, you two have met," Leo said and beamed with pride. "This is my amazingly talented and resourceful activities director, Thandie. She is responsible for such a successful inaugural week here."

Thandie saw Davis raise an eyebrow in suspicion as he looked around the area. A backhoe and bulldozer were working on the finishing touches of the new drainage system around the barn and down to the old dock. Long timbers had been placed across the ditch as a temporary access road. Construction and storm debris was piled high along the main road, and a machine with a large claw scooped and dropped the debris into a red dumpster.

Everywhere she looked, people were helping people, just like the folks from her hometown would have done. Though she felt no love for Davis, love was definitely in the air in all the ways that mattered. Davis's scowl, however, told another story. He would never get it. The only thing he would ever fully grasp was the bottom line. And a bottom line is what she would give him.

First, Thandie thanked Leo for his endorsement of her work there. Then she turned to Davis, taking his cheeks between her hands like she was going to plant one on him. "Davis, look at me. I'm only going to say this once and I want to be very clear. You listening?"

He nodded and smirked like a weasel, teeth all showing in the front over his lip. She let go of his face and stepped back.

"You came here at a really bad time, but I want you to see what's happening here. This resort is so much more than dollars. It's about a whole community and the way people come together in good times and in bad." She chose that phrase specifically to remind him of what he had broken between them. His eyes flinched ever so slightly at the reference, and she knew she had gotten to him. "And I don't care what Grant has to say. You trust me, and if it's the bottom line you want, this place is a gold mine. An untapped one. If you want to invest in The Foundry, then you give this wonderful man a fair shake. Don't do it for me though."

"But I did this for you. For us, Than."

"You can't buy my love like this." Thandie threw a look at Leo with her brows and a side nod. "I have something I need to take care of."

Leo, catching onto what she was getting at, took over. "Thank you Thandie. She's correct. This storm aside, I know we have something special here. An untouched market in the area, coupled with the growing trend of folks getting out of the city to have a one-of-a-kind experience."

Davis stopped him. "I'm a numbers man. So, let's see it, and I'll try and ignore all the mess in the meantime," Davis said and turned to Thandie. "And I still want the full report from Grant."

Thandie nodded to Leo, and he took Davis towards the loft office. It was an unsaid understanding that they were on the same mission. Meanwhile, ignoring her obvious issues with Davis, she knew that Leo still needed and deserved the investment. The plan was simple: convince Davis to invest in the resort and work the rest out later.

Thandie turned to America. "Can you do me a favor?" she asked after the men had gone. "Whatever happens, can you keep Grant here? Don't let him leave."

"I'll try," she said with concern. "But why?"

"I'll tell you everything later," Thandie said as she began towards his cabin, hoping to find him there. "I promise."

Thandie used her sprinter's legs and ran down the still-sopping grounds at an unsafe pace. Words scrolled through her head at what she would say to him. She owed him an apology first and then an explanation about Davis.

His cabin wasn't far. She just hoped he was there. She slowed as she came around the front steps. Catching her breath, she leaned over with her hands on her knees. She hadn't run that quickly since high school and was now regretting not keeping up with it.

Up the steps, she hesitated on the stoop. Her hand pressed flat on the center of the door. She played out her words in her mind one last time before knocking. And knocking.

He wasn't there.

"Of course, you're not here," she said, remembering that he had moved all of his things to her cabin the previous night. She wasted no time and ran back to her place, where she found a gloomy-looking man who typically sported bright eyes and an unmatched, cheerful demeanor, sitting on the front edge of the wraparound porch. She hoped this time his demeanor was laced with forgiveness.

With his head buried in his hands, and his feet planted in the mud, he said, "What do you want?"

She walked the rest of the way to him, slow and deliberate in her steps. "Hey there," she said kindly.

His head stayed down. "I don't have a key." His voice sounded broken.

Thandie stopped in front of him. Her eyes shifted from the door and back to Grant. "I'm so sorry."

"Don't," he said and lifted his eyes to her. "You don't owe me anything."

"I know I don't," she said and sat beside him on the front steps. "I had no idea he was coming."

Grant sat up. "I did. But I didn't know my boss, Davis, is also *your* Davis. The one who you stacked stones for, and kicked and cried over. The one who I swore if I ever found out who he was, that I would—"

"What? Take him around the back of the barn and kick the snot out of him?"

"Sort of," he said and cracked a grin for a split second.

"It's not necessary. I meant what I said. I've let that all go."

"You forgave him?" Grant said and scooted his bottom a foot away from hers.

"Of course I did. How could I not?" She knew that she had to forgive what Davis did to her if she were ever going to be able to move on with someone else. And she thought Grant might be that someone. "I didn't mean for you to see that back there."

"You think that's what I'm mad about? That you forgave him and kissed him?" he said and stood up, pacing the front porch.

She was confused until he spoke.

"You had me going. All week long. You were just showing everyone so much attention because you knew one of us was here on behalf of the investor. I thought you and I—"

"I was doing my job." As soon as she said those words, she wished she hadn't. It sounded like the weakest excuse ever. "I don't mean it like that."

"Well, you did your job marvelously. I was having such a good time with you that I nearly forgot what I was even here for."

"That's right. When were you going to tell me that you worked for the investor and that you were here to spy on me?"

He paused.

"That long, huh? Did you think I wouldn't find out?" she said, her anger turning to hurt in her cracking voice.

He looked up and dabbed his face below his eyes. "I trusted you, Thandie."

"And I trusted you." She paused. Walking away and then back to him again. "Were you ever going to tell me?"

"I thought you knew who I was. At the bonfire the other night. You said you knew, and that we were done pretending."

"Pretending. I was talking about that I knew that you liked me. I knew that there was something wonderful growing between us, and that we were both healing our wounds. Together. I thought we had an understanding."

"And I thought you knew I was the spy, as you call it." Grant stood in front of the door. He palmed the knob and turned it. The door opened without the key he had said he needed. He grunted and went in.

"Where are you going?" Thandie followed him in. "You can't leave. Not yet. We're not done here."

"I think Davis would disagree with you. I'm guessing he's not done with you, and you've forgiven him anyway. You said it yourself." Grant walked into the bathroom and took his toiletries in the hem of his shirt. He tossed them in his bag, and a couple of items fell to the floor.

Thandie bent down to help, and their hands fell on the same little bottle. "Grant, you don't know what you're talking about. I did forgive him, and I did have a job to do, but that has nothing to do with us."

"Thandie, there is no us. You did your job well and—and I did mine." He stood and clapped, making her feel small. "Up until Mr. Mothan showed up, you had me convinced about this place. Now I don't know what to think."

There was nothing she could say that would change his mind. He was hurt or maybe jealous. But her job was on the line, a job that she desperately needed if she ever wanted to have a fresh start. But she was hurt, too. He had hidden who he really was because it was part of his job. And she had hidden behind her pride.

"I was doing my job. You aren't wrong about that," she said. "And now I need you to do yours. Davis needs your full report as soon as possible. I hope that you won't let this misunderstanding between us sway your assessment."

"How could it not, Thandie? Since I came here, you have been by my side. You helped me see that there was life past the scars in my life. And I trusted you."

"I really am sorry. About everything. Davis thinks he can invest in this place and win me back. Regardless of his reasons, you've made it very clear that you hold your job in high esteem.

So, be the professional you believe you are, but don't punish Leo on my account."

"I need some time."

Thandie knew there was plenty more work to do around the property and she was technically on the clock. "Please, convince Davis that this investment is worth it." She walked out the cabin door, unsure where to go next.

CHAPTER 25

Losing something often results in clarity, and this time was no different. Losing Davis had been devastating at the time. Though Thandie knew she didn't mourn the loss of him. She grieved for the idea of a happy marriage that he had stolen from her when he left.

She had only known Grant for a few days, and he already held a piece of her heart. A piece that she didn't know she had left to give to anybody. Now that she knew she was able to love again, she wasn't ready to discard the idea so easily. She only hoped that Grant could put aside what he saw as a betrayal and give an honest account to Davis about the state of the retreat.

In the meantime, there was work to do. In the distance, she saw America making her way to the cabin beside the one where Grant had stayed. "Hey, America, wait up," Thandie yelled across the open space outside.

America turned and waved Thandie over.

In no time at all, Thandie caught up to America. She didn't care what America's task was, she just needed to keep busy while Grant mulled over his report. There was nothing more she could do, and she hoped that the week's experience was enough alone for him to convince Davis to invest. Whoever was investing the money, she just wanted the business to succeed. Keeping down a job long enough to save the money needed to get back home was a benefit too.

"Do you need help? I don't even care what it is, I just need to get some of my energy out."

"That'd be great. Thanks."

"How are things going up there at the barn, anyway?" Thandie said as they made their way across the wet ground, stepping from dryer tufts of grass to others.

"I think they're nearly finished with all the repairs. Pa's fixing that window in the barn right now, the one that water was pouring through. I didn't see it, but Leo told me it looked like a faucet was on," America said. "Also, I have good news for you. It looks like next week's retreat is still going to happen, as long as we get these cabins turned over."

"What about the rooms with leaks?" Thandie knew of at least one cabin that needed roof fixes—Grant's—and by the quantity of downed limbs and scattered leaves, she was certain there were other structures that had been damaged in the storm too.

"We have the rest of today and tomorrow to get as many things fixed up as we can. Luckily, we only need three of the cabins, since most of the guests are in groups. I have the binder ready for you at my house." America rambled as they went inside the little bungalow and kicked off their muddy boots.

Thandie hadn't had time during her first day to check out all the different accommodations, and this one was darling. Leaving her dirty shoes by the door, she opened all the drapes and let the late afternoon sun filter into the space. She stood in the quaint, English-inspired cottage with its floral wallpaper and painted furniture. Little accents of gold and iron dotted the living room and kitchen area, complete with glossy, white enamel appliances.

The design was so unlike the cabin she was staying in, and nothing like the one where Grant had stayed either.

"I'll start with the linens in the primary," America said, which reminded Thandie of her first night's stay in the most perfectly made bed.

"You think you can show me your trick sometime?"

"What trick?" America said from the bedroom.

Thandie gathered the kitchen towels and a blanket from the couch and threw them into a pile near the door. "How you make the beds so expertly. The sheets were soft but taught, and the covers were just the right amount of cozy and warm."

America chuckled. "I agree. But I'm not the one you should ask. Leo is the magician with all the bed-making skills."

"Seriously?" Thandie said, supposing her gender bias had caused her to assume America was the one who made the beds.

A loud thud vibrated the floor beneath Thandie's toes. Rounding the corner into the bedroom, she stifled a giggle with the back of her hand at the sight. America stood waist deep in linens and was barely visible behind a shower of feathers.

"What happened in here?"

"The pillow seam blew out when I took the case off," America laughed and sunk down to the floor.

Thandie joined America on the ground and watched the little white feathers fall around them. When the giggles subsided, they just lay there for a moment, as though they each needed a tiny break from the disaster outside.

"Do you want to tell me what was going on between you, Mr. Mothan, and Grant a little while ago?" America asked and broke the silence. "And don't tell me nothing. I know that look in your eyes from when we were up at the barn. Spill it."

Thandie had nothing to lose by telling America the truth, though she was a little afraid of hearing the truth out loud. "I think I'm in love with Grant."

"And you're worried because you just met him?" America said but continued talking before Thandie could answer. "Did anyone tell you about me and Leo? We met, fell in love, and were engaged all in a few weeks. Time doesn't mean anything when you find your person. So, don't be scared."

"That's not exactly the problem," Thandie said and waved her hands in the air, moving the feathers around in swirls. "Remember when I told you that my fiancé left me the day before the wedding?"

"Yes," she said like a question.

"The man who broke my heart is Davis."

"No!"

"Yes! And what's worse, Grant is his consultant. Believe me, I had no idea about him or the investor or any of it when I took this job—"

"Of course, you couldn't have known," America said.

"Thank you for that. But to make things worse, Grant thinks that Davis and I are getting back together."

"Why would he think that?"

Thandie sat up and moved to the end of the mattress. "He caught Davis kissing me up at the barn."

"Did you kiss him back?"

Thandie squirmed from the thought, and America raised an eyebrow.

"On top of that," Thandie stood up and rung her hands together, preferring pacing over sitting, "when I asked him to give an honest report, he basically accused me of trying to sway his opinion with all the attention I showed him this week. Which is a mischaracterization."

"He feels betrayed?"

"He feels like I lied all week and only spent time with him because it was my job." Thandie wiped a tear falling on her cheek. "It's true, I did try and show him the best of this place like I did for all the guests. The difference is that I was only looking forward to seeing *him* grinning back at me during every event and activity, not any of the other guests. From the moment he ran me over on the hiking trail the first day and held me in his arms, afraid that I was hurt badly, I wanted nothing more than to see him every day."

"Did you tell him how you feel?" America asked.

Thandie went to the bathroom where she collected the towels and bathmat. "I thought I did, but I doubt he believes me. He thinks that I'm in love with Davis and that everything that happened between us was fake."

"I don't know what to say, Thandie. The only advice I can give you is to tell him everything. From the start. And let him make up his own mind once he has all the facts."

America was speaking out of love and what sounded like experience. "Did you ever go through something like this before?"

America kicked the pile of linens towards the living room, and added them to the kitchen towels and throw-blanket. "I accused Leo of not caring about this community when he was the mayor. I thought he would never forgive me, but I told him the truth and let it be. Time provided some clarity for him and me both."

"What I need him to do now is write his report for Davis, secure the funding that you and Leo need, and then . . . I don't know."

"The truth, Thandie. You tell him the truth about how you feel. You tell him exactly what you told me. You tell him that you're not in love with Davis." America retrieved a bucket of cleaning supplies from under the sink and handed Thandie a duster and some disinfectant spray. "Does he know what happened between you and that awful man?"

"Not exactly. He knows that Davis hurt me in some way and that I forgave him."

"You did?" America started the water running at the sink.

"I can't move on unless I let go of what he did to me. Someone told me that moving on sometimes means starting over, and that's what I feel like I did this week. This place, the people, the guests, and Grant, all helped me see a future that I'm worthy of. I was able to see that life isn't a straight line that one can just plan out. Life isn't even a road. It's a flood, a disaster, that can be turned into something beautiful, something better."

"There's no perfect relationship, and it's something you have to fight for every day," America added and hit Thandie's sentiment right on. "Are you going to fight for Grant? Please tell me you are!" She clapped her hands together in excitement. "I love a good romance story."

Thandie smiled. "What else can a girl do?"

"Love with all her heart, no matter what." America took Thandie's hands and set her gaze on her face. "Let this thing finish with Davis, and then fight with all you have for Grant." She nodded, and Thandie reciprocated the gesture.

"Do you recall telling me that this place would be a safe harbor for me?" Thandie asked.

"Yes, why?"

"Because it has been. Thank you for that. For everything. No matter what happens after today, please know how grateful I am to you."

"Of course," America said. "You're welcome."

"Now, I know what I need to do," Thandie said.

As she completed her thought, the front door opened, and Leo came in. "Hey you two. I hoped I'd find you in here." He looked at Thandie. "I wanted to let you know that your phone is all fixed up." He handed it over. "Not that you'll get much of a signal, but I thought you'd like to have it back."

"I would love to have my phone back, actually." Thandie hugged it into her chest. "How did you get it fixed so fast, anyway? I thought I would need to buy a new one."

"I know a guy," Leo said. "Plus, you're going to need it if you're staying on as director past next week."

"Really? You got the funding?" America asked, smiling.

Leo rocked his head back and forth. "Well, it's looking good, but it's not locked in yet," he said and turned to America. "I believe in this project. Even without the money, we'll find a way. And I think Thandie needs to be a part of The Foundry."

Thandie nodded, words having left her mind.

"Plus, just think of all the help we got today with the cleanup. My brother? I mean, who would have thought that he, of all people, would come through?"

"Christmas Cove is part of John's community now too. Your success here looks good for the whole city," America said.

Leo nodded and Thandie saw him grin. Whatever was happening with Leo and his brother was the same sort of healing her own heart had undergone in the past week. Spring showers really can create beautiful change. The rain that she had been fighting against all week ended up bringing out the best in people. Even the guests had helped with the sandbagging effort. All that water washed away her past and caused something new to bloom within her: hope for the future and safety from life's storms.

"Hey, Leo. I think I finally have a name for the barn and you're both gonna love it."

"We're renaming the barn?" America asked, and Leo nodded. "Well?"

Thandie took a deep breath. "How about Harbour House? It fits with the lake theme, even if it does dry up. And people will feel what I've felt, that The Foundry is a safe place to heal, to grow, to explore . . ."

"To find love?" America asked.

"That too." Thandie said and tugged her boots on. Dried mud fell off and sprinkled on the ground. "I'll get that later. I have a phone call to make and a voicemail to listen to," she said and ran out.

Thandie sprinted toward her car and glimpsed Grant heading inside the Harbour House doors. He didn't look back or see her as she ducked inside the driver's side door.

CHAPTER 26

Following his conversation with Thandie and compiling his report, Grant took his time walking up to the barn. He gripped his report in his hand, even though he was still unsure whether he was doing the right thing. Never, in all of his years as a consultant, had he been in as much turmoil over a final judgment as he was now. He was good at his job, but his heart was tugging him in two opposite directions?

The long walk to the barn did nothing to ease his mind. He knew this retreat was a special place, and a few hours ago he was planning on giving the project a green light. But he knew Davis, or at least he knew many people just like him. Davis was a self-serving and ruthless venture capitalist who didn't care about the heart of a project, only the bottom line, and he had said as much earlier.

If Grant gave the investment a glowing review, would the firm's money mean that the retreat would become just like every other resort, where the life of it is quickly replaced by a spreadsheet? He didn't want that to happen. Not because of Thandie, or Leo, or any of the community that had all pitched in to clean up after the storm, but because his pain from the past was gone. This place, with its rolling hills and wildflower fields, had replaced his grief with hope in love.

Grant was still unsure as he walked inside and found Davis sitting at one of the square bistro tables. His head was buried in a computer screen, and a hands-free receiver covered one ear, the kind with the little mic part extending down his cheek. He looked like a prick. Davis had that confident swagger of a successful man and the good looks to top it off. Grant was certain that Thandie knew how handsome the man was too.

Guilt twisted Grant's stomach. He had spent much of the last decade striving to be more like the Davises of the world. Doing his job and doing it well with no apology. Spreadsheets and calculations had been his best friends, but during his recent consultations, he had failed to look at the heart of the project. Instead, he had focused too much on the numbers. It was clearer than ever that the numbers alone don't tell the whole story.

His spine straightened. This time, this project was going to be different.

"Mr. Mothan. I hoped to find you up here," Grant said and took a seat across the table from Davis. "You're enjoying the *cucina*?"

Davis looked around as though he hadn't taken in the space yet. His eyes came back to the computer screen. "You have my report?"

Grant's grip tightened around the rolled-up sheets of paper. "Sir, I think this investment . . . What I mean to say is—"

"Spit it out, Mr. Goldie."

"You shouldn't invest here." Grant felt relief at having made the decision, but a new panic arose from how he would explain his choice to Leo. He felt hot all over and fought the urge to pulse his tee shirt and let in some fresh air.

Grant's suggestion got Davis's attention. "Color me shocked," he said. "I was certain you were giving a good report. When we spoke over the phone, you sounded like you were in love with this place. What happened?"

What happened, indeed? Was it the storm, the cleanup, the kisses by the fire, the way Thandie looked after him when he overreacted—in more than one way—to the flower fiasco, or cooking hotdogs over the bonfire in the rain? Or was it the quiet moment of solitude where he thought about the woman he had once loved and how he felt free to think of his life without her for the first time since she passed away?

No, Grant thought, it wasn't one thing, it was the whole of it.

There was no part of his experience at the retreat that could have helped him heal by itself. Every single moment, each day, served to lessen his scars in some way. It was only a bonus that he had a wonderful, beautiful, and funny activities director that got him out of his walled castle and into a place of contentment.

"Grant," Davis whisper-yelled across the table. "I looked at the financials and I was ready to transfer the funds on Monday. What is the problem? You need to convince me."

"Honestly?"

Davis snapped back, "That's what I'm paying you for, isn't it?"

"I think an investment, yours, or anyone else's, would destroy this place. I think that if you give the money, you'll start to dictate how they use it and steer its use to things that will bring you more profit, and not necessarily toward what's best for the retreat." It felt good to say his thoughts out loud, though he wondered as Davis's smirk widened across his face if he had calculated incorrectly.

"That's quite presumptuous of you to assume I would ruin this place in pursuit of money," Davis said. "Your report, please?"

Grant crunched the papers in his hand. If Davis saw his report, he would surely make the deal with Leo. His report had nothing but positives, and every word of it was true. "No. I can't give it to you."

"You don't have your report prepared?"

Grant held it up beside his face and tapped the roll against his temple.

"Give it to me!" Davis raised his voice. "No report. No paycheck."

Grant was fine with this arrangement. "So be it." He stood and walked toward the trash can under the *cucina* sign. With each step, he tore the paper in half, and in half again. Ultimately, coming to a stop at the trash can and letting the papers fall from his hand like tickertape.

"What are you doing?" Leo yelled as he bolted inside the barn doors and caught the papers in his outstretched palms. "Is this the report? Is it that bad?"

"That's just what I was wondering," Davis said and looked at Grant. "You're fired! Get out of my face."

"Is that what you said to Thandie before you discarded her?" Grant turned to the man, who was no longer his boss, with an urge igniting inside of him to take Davis behind the barn and kick the snot out of him, just like Thandie had accused him of wanting to do earlier.

"Excuse me? You don't know what you're talking about."

Davis was correct, Grant didn't know any of the details, only that this man had walked out on Thandie. Blustering, he added, "You heard me!"

"First of all, she is none of your concern, and secondly, I apologized for leaving her the night before our wedding, and she forgave me."

Grant recalled his first meeting with Davis, when he had casually asked if Grant had ever left someone at the altar, *She forgave him anyway?* He felt terrible. No wonder Thandie had wanted to take things slower with him. She was still in love with another man. It was no wonder she was timid in opening up to him. It was no wonder that she refused help at almost every turn. She had only herself to rely on. Grant felt like a fool for not putting the pieces together earlier when it could have made a difference in how he had spoken to Thandie.

"The lesson here is about realizing that you've made a mistake and apologizing for it." Davis stood in front of Grant and patronized him like a parent scolding a child. "Would Grant like to apologize and get his job back?"

"No! Grant would not like his job back," Grant said in a mocking tone.

"You'll never get another job again if I have—"

Grant stopped him short. "This has nothing to do with me apologizing for telling the truth. It has to do with someone that has so much love in her heart that she can even forgive the unforgivable. Neither one of us deserves her."

Davis spun around on his heels and poked a finger into Grant's chest. "Wait a minute. You're in love with my fiancée?"

"Of course not! What an absurd thing to say. Like you said, she's your fiancée, and she has forgiven you. I'm nobody." Grant knew the words coming from his mouth weren't the whole truth, but not lies either. "I hope you will do right by her. And whatever you decide about The Foundry, don't hold my actions against Leo. He is a good person, and this place is amazing." Grant turned to walk out and saw America standing by the door, wiping tears from her cheek.

He walked past her and through the doors, and she followed him out.

"What the hell are you doing?" America said and stomped down the drive after him. "Hey! I'm talking to you."

"What do you want?" he snapped.

Her hands went up in a show of peace. "Whoa. You need to take it down a bit. I'm not the enemy here."

She wasn't, but the overwhelming urge to punch that man, Davis, in the face was taking every last ounce of self-control that Grant had left. He just wanted to get out of there and put this whole thing behind him.

"Where are you going?" she asked.

"My job is done. You probably heard that I'm fired, so I'm leaving."

"From what I heard back there, you fired yourself." America closed the distance between them, and he could see the softness in her eyes. Her genuine concern for him relaxed the tension in his shoulders. "What did you end up telling Mr. Mothan?"

"I told him not to invest."

"Are you serious! How could you? This week was perfect. Except the rain and—"

Grant interrupted her rambling. "This week was perfect."

His words shut her up as she processed what he said. "Then why—"

"If you get his money, everything special about this place, and it is very special, will change. So, I told him not to invest." Grant kicked the gravel in his path. "It wasn't an easy thing for me to do. But you don't want a guy like that anywhere around here."

"I suspect not," America said and kicked the gravel too. "And that's why he fired you?"

"I wouldn't give him my report, because I knew if he read it that he would jump on the opportunity to be a part of this in a heartbeat. So, I tore it up and threw it away."

"And that's when Leo picked it out of the trash," she finished his thought. "I don't understand one thing, though."

"What's that?" he said.

"Why are you still standing here and not going after what you really want?"

What he really wants? How would this woman know anything of what he desired? He raised an eyebrow, coaxing her to continue her thought.

"I'm talking about Thandie."

He took an exasperated deep breath and blew it out. "You didn't hear? She forgave Davis, and I guess they're back together now. I even caught them kissing earlier."

"Are you daft?" America sucker punched him in the shoulder with surprising force.

"Ouch," he moaned and held the sore spot in his hand.

"She forgave him because she's ready to move on and didn't want to carry that baggage into her next relationship. A relationship she hopes will be with you."

"Me?"

"So, if you're done being a fool—"

"Where is she?"

America pointed at the tire tracks still visible in the mud, heading away from the barn.

"Can I borrow your car?"

She tossed him the keys and pointed at the cherry-red pickup parked in the drive. "Go on."

CHAPTER 27

Thandie would have loved if her car could traverse the muddy roads any quicker. As it was, her tires seemed happy to be just moving at all, and so was she. She ran the wipers and dirty little splatters streaked across her field of view. As though the sticky strawberry guts weren't bad enough, now her wheel wells were encrusted with half-dried mud cakes.

Wishing for a nice drive-thru car wash, or enough money to spend on a good detailing, she rolled her window down and wiped the side mirror with the palm of her hand. The cool air rushed in, and she took a deep breath. The drive around the end of the lake was hard going. Between the washed-out sections that created giant speed bumps, and the downed limbs scattered along the eastern shoulder, she wasn't sure how long it would take for her to get to the overlook. The same overlook where she had first met Grant and fallen in love with the Cove.

Now that her job was secure, at least for a time, she suspected she would spend many more days taking in the scenery around The Foundry. In a million years, she would not have guessed that being an activities director would have suited her so well. Though she had always enjoyed connecting with people, it had never occurred to her to lean into that part of her personality for work's sake.

Now that it had, it was hard to imagine doing anything else. She had doubted she would stay in Christmas Cove for very long, though her experience that week was the first in months that she truly felt was a fit. *Perhaps everyone should go on a solo road trip across the country, take on different jobs, and see what sticks*, she wondered. It had worked for her.

No matter what the future held, she wouldn't let herself fall in love with any more guests. She had made this mistake once and couldn't afford to do it again. It had been improper of her to spend so much alone time with Grant, even if Leo had asked her to make sure everyone of the guests had a good time. She was the one who pushed the boundaries with Grant.

It was her decision to take off her clothes and get into the spa with him. The rain was just a sweet excuse that she took full advantage of. Maybe she would have never suggested it herself, but she was excited by the idea of sharing such an intimate experience with him. Her body ached at the thought of seeing him each day. And she hoped she would get a chance to speak with him before he departed, even if it was only to say goodbye.

"So, what you're saying is that you love him?" JB's voice carried through the car, and Thandie nearly forgot that her friend was still on the line.

"I didn't say that."

"You didn't have to," JB said with a giggle. "I can't believe you stayed up all night just talking. I don't think I could have done that. It's the sweetest thing I've ever heard. What a gentleman!" she said and swooned.

Thandie swerved around a pothole, and the car bumped along the edge of it. "Woah. That was close."

"You alright?" JB asked.

"Yeah. The roads are a mess," Thandie said. It was nice to talk to a familiar friend.

"I'm surprised you're even getting service at The Foundry."

"I'm heading up the hill to the overlook," Thandie said. "I figured I might get a better signal from up here. When I called you, I didn't know whether it would go through or not."

"I'm glad you called, but I can't be the only reason you're heading up the hill."

"I met Grant near the overlook, and I thought going back there could give me some clarity. And I wanted to check in and see how you fared after the storm."

"We did alright. My property is sloped enough to keep the buildings dry," JB said. "I heard about the lake. Is it really holding water?"

From her vantage point on the ridge, Thandie could see the water glistening in the late day sun. Little ripples seemed to glow like fireflies in summer and roll out towards the shore. "It looks pretty full to me. It'll be a while before that amount of water dries up."

"I bet the roads aren't much better. Will you be careful up there?" JB said, and not a moment too soon.

Thandie drove through a puddle and the car skidded off the road onto the muddy shoulder. She put the car in a lower gear and pressed the gas pedal. The car didn't budge. She threw the gears into reverse and tried easing herself out, but the tires just rotated, spraying thick, brown muck into the air around her car.

"I'm stuck."

"It's okay for you to not know what to do next. Just think about it before making any rash decisions," JB said.

Thandie laughed. "No, I mean, I appreciate your advice, but I'm physically stuck. In the mud. The car won't move."

It was JB's turn to laugh. "I see. That is very different."

"I'm gonna get out and see what I can do. Stay on the line?" Thandie asked and opened the driver's side door.

Her feet sank into the mud and sucked at her boots. Each step felt like she was walking in quicksand with sacks of flour tied around her ankles. She did a quick survey of the area around the car. If she could pull some old bush branches and some long grass out and throw it down behind the tires, she could gain some traction.

It was the only plan, short of waiting for a good Samaritan to come along with a winch or tow. As she was alone on this particular stretch of road, she took long, heavy steps through the muddy area to where the ground had better drainage and was actually walkable.

She gathered the loose stuff first and tossed it up near the car's rear tires until a decent pile had covered the mud. Getting clumps of grass proved to be more difficult than she would have thought. Growing up on a farm, there was nothing she didn't know how to cut down, grass included. But this bright-green spring stuff wasn't giving up without a fight.

Thandie took a clump of the best-looking stuff, a foot and a half tall and six inches around, and gripped as tight as she could. She counted down.

Three.

Two.

One.

She locked her fingers and pulled as hard as she could. The grass gave up its hold, along with all the roots, and about a half a ton of soaked soil. Her momentum carried her backwards and directly into the sopping puddle beside her car.

She screamed and could hear JB's voice emanating from inside the car. Thandie couldn't hear exactly what her friend was saying, but answered the likely question. "Everything is fine!" Thandie yelled into the air. But it wasn't. The week was ending the way it had begun, with her ass in the mud again.

With an exasperated growl, she tossed the mud and grass down to the fence in front of her.

The sun was setting fast, and the fields in the distance glowed bright yellow and green. Further away, the flowers danced in shades of muted blue hues along the horizon. It would be a beautiful scene to take in if it weren't for her being suctioned in place forever.

Already covered in mud, she flopped back and laid in it with her arms outstretched. "This is it. This is how I die."

The situation was far from serious, but with how exhausted she was, dying seemed like the easiest way to get some rest. Or at least, laying there for a moment or two could be nice.

Before she could perish in her own puddle of hopelessness, headlights came around the corner downhill from her, bumping up and down with the dips in the road. The car most likely hit the same pothole she had run across before finding herself in her current situation. She sat up, but the shifting of her weight forward captured the whole of her bottom in the mud, and clumps of slimy dirt slid down the back of her white shirt. Deciding that she did not, in fact, want to kick the bucket just yet, Thandie reached for a clod of earth and threw it up into the air as the vehicle approached.

The old, red pickup truck, slowed down, having seen her distress signal. Relieved, she laid back again and awaited rescue. "Careful, this stuff is super sticky," she said to her would-be hero.

"Why is it that you are always covered in mud?"

It was Grant. Her heart skipped a beat at the sound of his sultry, low voice, though she detected humor there. Whether from embarrassment or absolute fatigue, tears pushed at her eyes.

"Why are you here?" she said with a shaky voice.

"For you," he said and stood in the mud over her. "Though, I admit, I didn't expect to find you in such a state."

"Stuck in the muck?" she said and threw a handful of mud into the brush.

"No," he said and sat down next to her. She tried protesting, but it was too late. His bottom was stuck right there beside hers. "Sad. I didn't expect to find you sad."

"I'm not sad," she said, as the tears fell freely. "I'm just . . . tired."

Grant took her chin and turned her face towards his. "It's more than that."

She nodded and tried to smile.

"Tell me."

This was the moment that America had prepared her for. It was time to fight for him. For Grant. Through her whimpering, she eked out three little words.

"Help me up."

"Not until you talk to me." He planted his feet in the mud, and she cringed at the thought that they might both be stuck there forever. She might as well get it over with.

"I love you," she said. The words felt sweet, like icing coming off her tongue. "I don't know what else to say . . ."

"You need a shower," he said and stood up with ease. He took her hands and helped her to her feet. Looking into her eyes, unwavering in his intensity, he nudged her head back with the back of his forefinger. His lips landed on hers, barely pressing into her, as though he was mapping their every curve.

She froze, not out of fear, but she had never felt so much passion in such a small act. She let him have her how he wanted in that moment. His dirty hands came around the small of her back and he pulled her waist against his body until no space existed between them.

Grant cradled her head with one hand, playing in the curly tendrils that had fallen out of her ponytail, and pressed his mouth against hers again. His lips fit with hers and they moved in rhythm together, neither taking nor giving more than the other. All their kisses leading up to this one had been merely practice. This one was the real thing.

When she needed air, she pulled back and broke their bond. Her eyes remained closed as she breathed him in. The air was thick and fragrant from the evaporating rain, and his body was hard beneath her fingertips.

"I love you too," he said.

"You do?" Her question wasn't one rooted in true disbelief that he was capable of loving her, but in how proudly he said it. "I love you, Thandie. I want everyone to know it!"

She kissed him quickly and backed away, looking around. "There are a couple of problems with that."

"I can get us out of this mud," he said.

"Yes, that is one obstacle, perhaps the most pressing," she said and moved her feet toward the pile of sticks behind her car. She crushed them down into the mud with her boot. "My ex-fiancé is your boss, and Leo said that he's probably investing in The Foundry."

"Ex-boss. Davis fired me," Grant laughed out.

"Fired you, for what?"

"For failing to fulfill my contracted duties. I told him not to invest here."

"Wait, why?" Thandie asked and could feel her anger rising in her chest.

"I don't want this place to become a cookie cutter corporate project where they only care about the good-old dollar. This place is too good for that."

"I think Davis was only interested in this place because he thought he could win me back. But really, I think he was just lonely after he got dumped."

"Dumped? By whom?"

"Bianca from Vegas. His affair didn't go so well." Thandie laughed at the irony.

"They never do, do they?" Grant chuckled.

"Either way, Leo needs the money. And I need the job."

"They'll get it. Somehow, I know it," he said, and she had no doubt he was telling the truth. "Just think about how far we've both come this week. If this place can help us heal and forgive, and open our hearts again, I want everyone to have an experience as powerful as that."

The truth was hard to argue against. Leo might have something to say about Grant sabotaging his chances at getting that money, but that really wasn't her concern. She had clearly done the job she was brought in to do, and she'd done it a little too well. The evidence was standing starry-eyed in front of her, and smeared with sticky dirt and verdant grass stains with mud just like she was.

There was something she needed to get off her chest, though. She took a deep breath, knowing what more she needed to confess. "Davis broke up with me the night before our wedding. I'm sorry. I should have told you this earlier—"

He put a finger over her lips. "I already know."

"You do? How?"

"He told me, though I didn't know he was talking about you at the time. And I don't blame you for not saying outright what happened. There you were, forgiving him and moving on, and I was thinking the worst about the whole thing. I don't know how you did it, forgiving him, but I understand why you felt like you needed to. You're strong, Thandie, and you must know that none of it was your fault."

"All I did was love him. He was the one who didn't show up. He was the one who called from Vegas to say, and I quote, 'I just can't.' I mean, who does that?" she said. "I suppose there was a part of me that always knew we weren't good together. He's a taker and I'm a giver. He sees his career as the pinnacle of what life has to offer, and I see the beauty in the world around me. And it's enough for me." She held Grant's hands. "After the last few days with you, something stirred in my heart that showed me who I really am, and I know I'm worthy of true, real love."

"And I know I have so much love to give. If you'll have me?" Grant leaned in to kiss her, but held back just a breath away from her lips, as though he were waiting for an answer.

"I will have you, Grant Goldie. Today and tomorrow, and the day after that, and the day after—" He stopped her sequence with his lips pressing against hers. She could feel him smiling through their kissing, and she tried not to giggle at how cute he was.

Clapping came from somewhere nearby and interrupted their kiss. Thandie paused. "Do you hear that?" she mumbled while their lips were still touching. "Clapping? Crying?"

"I'm just so happy," JB's voice sounded from Thandie's phone, still sitting on the dashboard inside the car, and Thandie covered her mouth with the back of her hand.

"Who is that?" Grant asked.

"I totally forgot. That's my friend JB. She's been on the speakerphone this whole time." Thandie stepped around to the driver's side with heavy boots weighed down with sticky mud. "I'm so sorry, JB!"

"I'm not," she said and sniffled. "That was the most beautiful thing I've ever heard."

Grant came around the car. "Hi, JB. I'm Grant."

"Grant Goldie, I know. Pleasure to meet you," JB said. "Congratulations, you two."

"Thanks," Thandie said. "Can I call you later?"

"Does this mean you're not going home anytime soon?" JB asked as Thandie was about to hang up.

"I think I am home," she said and disconnected the call.

With her feet planted in the mud, and her hands around Grant's waist, they kissed again. This time with a tenderness that comes from two people who understand the journey to healing that she and Grant shared. They had both weathered storms, and now they could grow a new and beautiful life together.

RATE AND REVIEW

We hope you enjoyed *Spring Showers* by Sarah Dressler. If you did, we would ask that you please rate and review this title. Every review helps our authors.

Rate and Review: Spring Showers - Christmas Cove Book 2

MEET THE AUTHOR

Sarah Dressler, author of the popular holiday romance series, Christmas Cove, calls the mountains of Colorado home, where she enjoys sunset walks with her husband of nearly twenty years and raising two very busy teens. Beginning her writing career as an award-winning fashion blogger, Sarah now writes fiction full time. Inspired by her father's military service and later as a military spouse, she pens novels that aim to reach a greater understanding of the world. With her appreciation for diverse cultures, Sarah's stories touch on themes of family, personal growth, and new beginnings in an uplifting and heartwarming manner.

OTHER TITLES FROM 5 PRINCE PUBLISHING